CORPORAL MAIDEN BARBARA WHITLEY, WING LEADER OF THE CROSSBOW CAVALRY, WAS NOT VERY PIOUS.

But before her stood a spaceship. This was Mystery. They had always said it; they sang it in the ritual, and as little girls they told it to each other on rainy nights when the fires leaped high on the barrack hearths: *Some day the Men will come to claim us.*

How would Barbara know if it was a Man, or one of the Monsters from space Men were said to have dealings with? The legends said, "Men are taller and stronger than we, infinitely wiser and more virtuous. They have hair on their chins and no breasts."

spotted lost space-explorer Davis Bertram. As realized the question

POUL ANDERSON
VIRGIN PLANET

WARNER BOOKS

A Warner Communications Company

WARNER BOOKS EDITION

Copyright 1959 by Poul Anderson
Copyright 1960 by Galaxy Publishing Corp.

ISBN 0-446-88334-4

This Warner Books Edition is published by
arrangement with Thomas Bourgey & Co., Inc.

Cover art by Charles Moll

Warner Books, Inc., 75 Rockefeller Plaza, New York, N.Y. 10019

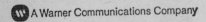 A Warner Communications Company

Printed in the United States of America

Not associated with Warner Press, Inc. of Anderson, Indiana

First Printing: May, 1970

Reissued: May, 1977

10 9 8 7 6 5 4

CHAPTER I

Corporal Maiden Barbara Whitley of Freetoon, hereditary huntress, wing leader of the crossbow cavalry and novice in the Mysteries, halted her orsper and peered through a screen of brush. Breath sucked sharply between her teeth.

She had come down the wooden mountain slope by a route circling south of town. The forest ended before her, as cleanly as if an axe had cut it, and the hills rolled away in a blaze of green and of red firestalk blossoms, down to the wide valley floor. Behind her and on either side the Ridge lifted, bending toward the north to form a remote blue wall; she could just see the snow on those peaks and the thin smoke of a volcano. Ahead, nearly on the horizon, was a line of trees and a metallic flash beneath low suns, telling where the Holy River poured to the sea.

Tall white clouds walked in a windy sky. At this time of day and year, when midsummer approached, both suns were visible. The first, Ay, was a spark so bright it hurt the eyes, sinking down the western heaven; the second, Bee, was a great gold blaze ahead of Ay, close to the edge of her world. Minos was waxing, huge and banded, in its eternal station a little south of the zenith. The moon Ariadne was a pale half-disc, shuttling swiftly away from the planet. By daylight the inmost moon Aegeus, tiny hurried star-point, was not visible . . . but the six hours of night to come would be light.

It was on the thing in the valley, five kilometers away where the foothills ended, that Barbara Whitley focused her gaze.

The thing stood upright, aflash with steel pride, like a lean war-dart, though it lacked fins. As a huntress and ar- balester, the corporal was necessarily a good judge of spa-

5

tial relationships, and she estimated its height as forty meters.

That was much smaller than the Ship of Father. But it was nearly the same shape, if the hints dropped by initiates were truthful. And it *must* have come from the sky.

A chill went along her nerves. She was not especially pious: none of the Whitleys were, and keeping them out of trouble had been one reason for making them all huntresses in peacetime. But this was Mystery. They had always said it; they sang it in the rituals, and they told it to children on rainy nights when the fires leaped high on the barrack hearths . . .

Some day the Men will come to claim us.

The orsper shifted clawed feet and gurgled impatiently. The creak of leather and jingle of iron seemed thunderloud to Barbara Whitley. "Father damn you, hold still!" she muttered, and realized with a shudder that her habit of careless profanity might call down wrath from the Men.

If this was the Men.

She could not see any movement about the dart-thing. It rested quiet in the valley, and the stillness of it was somehow the most unnerving of all. When a gust of wind rustled the leaves above her, Barbara started and felt sweat cold under the leather cuirass.

Her hand strayed to the horn slung at her waist.

She could call the others. When the shining object had been seen descending this morning, with none who could tell what it was or just where it had landed, Claudia, the Old Udall, had sent out the whole army to search. She, Barbara, had chanced to be the one who found it. (Or was there such a thing as chance where the Men were concerned? Or was this a ship of the Men at all?) There must be others within earshot, perhaps already watching.

The Old Udall had given no specific orders. That was unlike her, but this was too unprecedented. There was, to be sure, an implication that the first scout to locate the unknown should report back immediately, but . . .

This might be a vessel of the Monsters. The Monsters were half folk-tale; it was said that they lived on the stars, and Men had dealings with them—sometimes friendly, sometimes otherwise.

A stray lock of rusty-red hair blew out from under Barbara's helmet and tickled her nose. She sneezed. It seemed to crystallize something in her.

Now that she thought about it, there must be Monsters in that ship, if it was a ship. The Men would arrive much more portentously, landing first at the Ship of Father and then at the various towns. And there would be haloes and such-like about them, and creatures of metal in attendance . . . well, there ought to be. And prodigies—didn't the Song of Barbara One-Eye, in speaking of her own ancestress and the raid on Highbridge, say: "And Minos shall dance in the sky when the Men pass by?"

It wasn't a canonical epic, but it dealt with a Whitley, so it must hold more truth than the Udalls and the Doctors would admit. They were a lot of old hags anyway.

Corporal Barbara Whitley was rather frightened at the idea of Monsters—she felt her heart thump beneath the iron breastshields—but they *were* less awesome than Men. If she went meekly back to town, she knew exactly how Claudia Udall would take charge in her own important way. The army would be gathered and move according to tactics which were, well, simply *rotten,* like the time when it had been led directly into a Greendale ambush. And a mere corporal, even though a wing leader, would be just nobody.

Barbara had never needed much time to reach her own decisions. She checked her equipment with rapid, professional care. The cuirass was on tight and the kilt-strips covered her thighs to the knee; below them, boots protected the calves and feet. Her morion was secure on her head, and the blue cloak firmly pinned. The axe at her saddle had been sharpened only yesterday; her dagger was keen and her lasso oiled. She cocked the repeating crossbow and tucked it in the crook of her left arm. Her right hand lifted the reins, and she clucked to the orsper.

It trotted forward, out of the woods and into the open, down the hill at the swift rocking pace of its breed. The blue-and-white feathers lay sleek and the great head, beaked and crested, with fierce yellow eyes, was sternly lifted. Barbara hoped she wouldn't have trouble—the orspers were brave enough when they understood conditions, but apt to squawk and run when something new appeared.

7

"Well, my girl," she said to herself, "here we go and Father knows what'll happen. I do hope it's only a crew of friendly Monsters." The Whitleys all had a way of speaking their thoughts aloud, another reason why they belonged to the noncom caste. A town chief or officer had to be more discreet.

The wind blew in her face, murmuring of the sea and the Ship whence it came. The sun Bee was almost in her eyes, so she began a circling movement to approach the dart-thing from the west. She imagined a hundred scouts watching her in admiration from the forest. But her fellow Whitley couldn't be among them—obviously—otherwise she'd be riding right along with her. A good thing, too! That little witch Valeria already had too much unearned credit.

Still no motion from the object—not a sound, not a stirring. Barbara grew quite convinced that there were Monsters aboard. Men would have been out long ago. And she could talk to a Monster—or fight it—at the worst, be killed by a thunderbolt, or whatever they used for weapons. Monsters had unknown powers, but they were still of this universe. Whereas Men . . .

Barbara had never thought a great deal about the Men. The songs and sayings she had had to learn had gone smoothly across her tongue without really penetrating her brain. "The Men are the males of the human race. We were coming to join the Men, but the Ship went astray because of our sins. The Men are taller and stronger than we, infinitely wiser and more virtuous, and they have hair on their chins and no breasts. . . ." She realized now that she had always vaguely thought of a Man as being like a very big woman, in fact, like her dimly remembered mother.

Once, when they were all little girls, Elinor Dyckman had tried to draw a picture of a Man, breastless and with hair on his face. The Dyckmans drew well, but the picture had been so silly that Barbara broke into giggles.

Now, as she rode toward the ship, the memory returned and another unholy fit of humor came on her. She was laughing aloud, above all the tension and wariness, as she reached the vessel.

"Hoy, there!"

She cried it forth, and heard her voice faintly shivered back from polished metal. No answer. A flock of gray rangers went overhead, calling to each other, incredibly unconcerned.

"Hoy! Corporal Maiden Barbara Whitley of Freetoon speaking! I come in peace. Let me in!"

The ship remained smugly silent. Barbara rode around it several times. There was a circular door in the hull, out of her reach and smoothly closed. She yelled herself hoarse, but there was not a word of reply, not a face in any of the blank ports.

Really, it was too much to bear!

She whipped the crossbow to her shoulder and fired a bolt at the door. The missile clanged off; it left no mark. The orsper skittered nervously, fluttering useless wings. For a moment Barbara was afraid of death in reply, but nothing happened.

"Let me in!" she screamed.

Now she was in a fuming temper. She loosed another futile bolt and blew her horn as loud as she could. A runner started from the long grass and dashed toward the river, its tail feathers wagging ridiculously. Barbara shot at it—a miss, and at such a range.

No wonder the stories said never trust a Monster!

Bee was very low now, the western clouds turning saffron and shadows marching across the valley. Ay was still high, but Ariadne had moved and Minos grown noticeably fuller. Streaks of mist floated above the forests of the eastern mountains.

The startled screech of the orsper jerked Barbara back to reality. There was someone running from the west.

Barbara could not see the person very well . . . yes, it had human form, it was not a Monster. On the other hand, it was not dressed like any townswoman she had ever heard of. It wore some kind of tunic; the legs were sheathed in cloth; there was a small packsack on the shoulders, and . . .

She spurred the orsper forward. "Hoy-aaah!" she called. "What in the name of ruin are *you* doing here?"

The stranger stopped. Barbara got near enough to see that it was a remarkably ugly person. The broad shoulders were not unpleasing, but the hips were grotesquely narrow. There was yellow hair cropped short, and a lean face with too much nose and chin, altogether too much bone and too little flesh.

Father! Maybe it *was* a Monster!

Thoughts runneled through her head as she dashed toward the being. It was certainly no member of any town, any family—she knew what all the five hundred families looked like, and while some were homely enough, none were so bad. Nor did any townsfolk on this side of Smoky Pass dress in that fashion. And it was approaching the ship . . . must have been looking around outside when she came, yes, that copse would have hidden it from her—and it was *deformed*!

She remembered from the old stories that Monsters had many shapes but some of them looked like deformed humans.

A single Monster!

Squinting into the sun-glare, Barbara saw that it had drawn something from a holster. A small tube, clutched in one hand and aimed at her . . . She whirled around to get the sun out of her eyes and saw that the crimson tunic was open at the neck, the chest was flat and hairy and there was thick hair on the arms . . .

Then she hardly had time to think. The Monster might or might not be peaceful. She couldn't simply down it with a crossbow bolt. At the same time, she wasn't going to be shot down herself like a sillyhead on its nest.

She released her grip on the bow and let it swing free from its shoulder strap. Her knees guided the leaping orsper and her hands whirled up the lariat.

The Monster stood there gaping. Its weapon tried to follow her skilled movements, the jumps and dashes meant to throw off an enemy aim. It took a deep breath and she heard words of her own language, but distorted, alien: "Cosmos in All, what's going on here?"

Then the lasso snaked out and fell around its body. The orsper sprang away, rope whirred through the hondo and the noose pinned arms to side.

Corporal Maiden Barbara Whitley galloped in triumph toward Freetoon, dragging the Monster behind her.

CHAPTER II

The episode had begun a couple of weeks earlier, and nearly two hundred light-years away.

All aglisten in fashionable tunic and culottes, boots polished to bedazzlement, Davis Bertram vaulted up the steps of the Coordination Service building. The morning sparkled around him and the raw ugliness of a new city on a new planet seemed only a boisterous good cheer. The door opened for him; he patted it kindly and strode into the lobby. His soles clashed on the floor and his whistling resounded in the corridors.

Smith Hilary was making feeble attempts to get information from the desk robot. He gave Davis a bloodshot look and said something about mutants with lead-lined stomachs and no soul at all.

"Merely virtuous living, and high thinking," said Davis Bertram. "Have you tried aneurine?"

"I've tried every pain killer known to human and non-human science," groaned Smith. "But after last night—*what* were we drinking?"

Davis warbled a popular song in reply.

"I hope the gobblies get you," said Smith. With a bleary malice: "Are you sure you can stand a month in space all by yourself?"

"No," admitted Davis blandly. "But then, I don't expect to. I expect to discover a planet full of beautiful women and stay for years. Is the Cosmic All at home?"

"The office opened an hour ago," said Smith. "If he didn't arrive on the dot, there must have been a supernova to stop him. Go away. I hope he eats you."

Davis threw him his beret and went on down the hall. A thousand light-years from Sol, on the edge of the known and settled by humans for barely two generations, Nerthus

11

was the local Cordy headquarters, and you had to get clearance from them. A stellagraphic voyage meant the chief's personal okay.

The door identified him and opened. Coordinator Yamagata Tetsuo occupied a large office, with a full-wall transparency to show him the spires of Stellamont and the plains beyond. He nodded curtly, a man grown bleak in a lifetime's war against the universe. "Sit down, Citizen," he invited. "You're two days overdue."

"I was in bed all the time. Quite a high temperature."

Yamagata gave him a sharp look. There was always the danger of a new disease on a new planet. "What diagnosis?" he snapped.

"Nothing reportable, sir," said Davis meekly. As a matter of fact, the organism reponsible was 1.6 meters tall, with blue eyes and a high center of gravity, but he saw no reason to mention that.

"Well . . ." The gaunt face remained expressionless. Yamagata pressed a stud and asked the infomaster for the Davis file. The machine grumbled to itself and spat the papers up onto the desk. The Coordinator riffled them with thin fingers while Davis fidgeted.

"Yes, I remember now. You were educated on Earth." The old man's eyes went outward, toward the sky, as if he would pierce its blinding blue and look across a thousand light-years to an unforgotten home. "Moved to Thunderhouse for astronautical training. Why?"

A flush crossed Davis' lean, somewhat too sharp features. He was a tall blond young man—a rare sight these days—with an athletic slenderness of which he was well aware. "I wanted to, uh, see a different planet. I'd only been in two systems, Sigma Hominis Volantis where I was born and then Sol. Variety—stimulus . . ."

"Hm. The Earth academy is the strictest in the known Galaxy, and Thunderhouse's is notoriously slack. Well, I'm afraid that's technically none of my business. You have just been licensed for independent operation and you want to make a survey based on Nerthus. Your own spaceship, I see."

Davis shrugged. Even nowadays, a personal fortune meant something. A chap whose father had made a good

12

thing of it wasn't necessarily a wastrel, was he? Davis had never liked Earth much; he considered it a stodgy planet. Too bad Earth dominated the Union.

"I have no right to stop you," said Yamagata in a sour voice. "Not on the basis of this file. But a one-man expedition into deep space—one man with almost no practical experience— Look, there's a stellagraphic survey planned for the Fishbowl Cluster. Leaves in three weeks. Excellent crew, and the skipper is Hamilton himself. I could probably get you a berth."

"No, thanks," said Davis.

"But why do you want to go to Delta Wolf's Head? Of all the lunatic . . . You *know* there's a vortex in that area. That's precisely why it's never been visited."

The eagerness burst from Davis: "Then anything might be in there!"

"Including your own death. We can't send rescue parties, you know. Space is too big—they'd never find you. Nor do we have personnel to throw away."

"I've got a Mark XX cruiser, sir. Armed, robotic, it does everything but think."

"That's supposed to be your function."

"I know why you're worried, sir," said Davis. "You don't like these unsupervised expeditions because they're apt to be bad for any natives. If you look at my psychograph, you will see a high goodwill quotient. *I'm* not going to rob or murder anybody."

Yamagata shook his head impatiently. "All right, all right. Let's discuss your orbital plan."

It was simple. The vortex, an unusually big one, had made a region fifty light-years across unsafe for as long as men had been around here: almost six decades now. It was finally withdrawing from the area of the star Delta Capitis Lupi. The Service intended to explore that double sun in another two or three decades, when there would be no chance of disaster. They ran enough risks in the ordinary line of work without taking on even the smallest additional hazard. But as of this moment, the star could *probably* be reached. Davis planned to go there, make the standard preliminary survey of its planets, and return.

If there were intelligent natives, or an uninhabited

13

world suitable for colonization, Davis' Star would become a very proud blazon in the Pilot's Manual. If not, he had only lost a few weeks.

Looking at the young man across the desk, Yamagata sighed and wondered if Columbus had been such a headlong idiot.

"Very well," he snapped. "If you do not return, Citizen Davis, we'll have to assume the vortex got you after all."

"Or the natives."

"Doubtful. We know very well there is no race with atomic energy in that system. Our neutrino detectors would have spotted it long ago if there were. I presume you can handle primitives, and know the rules against getting too rough with them."

Davis nodded, a little sulkily. He had had vague notions about being the great white god to a grateful folk with tails and antennae . . . adolescent daydreams, of course; culture patterns deserved protection, could not be upset overnight without grave damage.

It would be enough to make the trip. If he did find an important planet—there was that girl over in the Jupiter Valley, and the glamor of a discoverer . . .

Yamagata stood up. "Good luck, Citizen," he said formally.

Davis bowed and went out. Yamagata heard him whistling as soon as he was in the corridor.

Presently Smith entered, to make a routine inquiry. He was a strictly interplanetary freightman, dealing with Hertha, the next world sunward. Yamagata stopped him. "You know that fellow Davis," he said. It was not a question.

"Yes. Uh, matter of fact, Coordinator, I was out on the town with him last night."

"Rich man's son." Yamagata stared through the wall. "Odd how things happen all over again on the frontier, isn't it? Phenomena like cities and private ostentation, that Earth outgrew a long time ago. Sometimes I wish only Solarians could be licensed to pilot spacecraft. The people who emigrated were those who didn't like the restraints of being civilized."

Smith waited, awkwardly.

14

"What do you think the boy's chances are?" asked Yamagata.

"Eh? Oh . . . pretty fair, I'd say. He's a natural-born pilot, has a good mind when he cares to use it. And he's got a fireball of a ship."

"He'll have to have a lot knocked out of him," said Yamagata. "I hope the process isn't fatal."

CHAPTER III

The *At Venture* lifted noiselessly on gravity beams, and the sky darkened and Nerthus became a great cloudy shield in a cold magnificence of stars. Davis Bertram let the autopilot do the work, plotting a course and steering it, and didn't bother to check the data. The robots were always right—almost always. He sat watching Carsten's Star dwindle and felt the loneliness close in.

At the appropriate distance, the ship went into hyperdrive and outpaced light, reaching for the Wolf's Head constellation. It would be about ten days to his goal.

He had intended to study advanced astrogational theory on the way. The tapes were there, and nothing to distract him; he couldn't even tune in a radio any more. But there was also a supply of stereofilms, and he might as well relax.

One of them looked interesting: *Murder Strikes Twice*. But it was from Earth, and turned out to be a symbolic verse drama in the ancient, rigidly stylized form of the Retribution. Davis swore and opened another spool.

On the third day he started his textbook work, and wrestled with the first problem given him for a good two hours. It was fun to start, but when he couldn't solve it he knocked off for a beer and somehow never got back to it. After all, he had a hundred and fifty years ahead of him, if the vortex didn't grab him off.

Conscientiously every watch, he set the internal field at two gravities and went through a routine of calisthenics. It bored him stiff, it always had, but a body in good trim was an asset.

Who had ever begun the idea that spacefaring was one long wild adventure?

Davis had spent enough time in flight, including the
16

cruises of cadet days, to know how empty the hours could become. But he had always vaguely assumed that on *his* ship it would be different.

He broke out his paints and brushes, set up a canvas, and started a portrait of Doris from memory. The art courses in the Earth schools had been among the few he really enjoyed. The academy on Thunderhouse had a mural of his in the messhall, a view from the inner moon.

It took him only a few hours to discover that painting a portrait of Doris from memory was a mistake. She had an interesting face, but the rest of her had been still more interesting. Davis suddenly realized he had spent nearly a whole watch period in reminiscences. He looked at the charcoal sketch he had made almost without thinking, blushed, and wiped his canvas clean. Too bad Doris wasn't here to pose. Only then he wouldn't be getting much painting done either. He recalled various psychopedagogues in his boyhood who had told him he must always be firm and upright, and brought his mind to heel. When he got back, rich and famous, there would be time enough for gynecological studies. Meanwhile, he'd better do something neutral, like a landscape.

Space itself, with no planets in view, nothing but a million unwinking stars and the great curdled rush of the Milky Way and the far cold coils of the galaxies . . . could not be painted. He was honest enough with himself to realize that.

On the eighth Earth-day, a frantic buzzing and a seasick quiver brought him out of his bunk, blind with panic. He had touched the vortex.

It wasn't close enough to matter. The thing was behind him in seconds. But he needed a depressor pill to stop shaking.

Uneasily, he looked up trepidation vortices in the Manual. It taught him nothing he didn't already know. For some little understood reason, there were traveling sections where the geometry of the continuum was distorted. The primary effect was that of violently shifting gravitational fields, and a big one could disturb a planet sufficiently to make the rotation period fluctuate by a few seconds. A spaceship on hyperdrive, its discontinuous psi functions meshing with those of the vortex, could be ripped to pieces—or flung a thouand light-years off course.

Space was unthinkably enormous. Even the largest vortex was not likely to encounter a ship by chance. But there had been vessels in the past, before the storms were known to exist, which had simply disappeared. There were suns and clusters today, interdicted because a vortex was in the neighborhood.

Well . . . this one hadn't hurt him. And it had saved Delta Capitis Lupi for his personal exploration!

CHAPTER IV

Minos was full, drenching Freetoon with cold amber light, and the air had grown chill. Barbara Whitley walked through silent streets, between darkened buildings, to the cavalry barrack. It formed one side of a square around a courtyard, the stables and arsenal completing the ring. Her boots thudded on the cobbles as she led her orsper to its stall.

A stone lamp on a shelf gave dim light, and the snoring grooms—all Nicholsons, a stupid family used only for menial work—stirred uneasily on the straw when she tramped in. She nudged one of the stocky, tangle-haired women awake with her toe. "Food," she demanded. "And water for the bird. Beer for me."

"At this hour?" grumbled the Nicholson. "I know my rights, I do. You soldiers think you can barge in at all hours, when honest folk is asleep after a hard day's work, and—" Barbara smiled, drew her dagger, and felt its edge in an absent-minded way— "oh, very well, very well, ma'am."

Afterward Barbara undressed and washed herself in the courtyard trough. Not all the girls were so finicky, but she was a Whitley and had appearances to keep up. She regarded her face complacently in the water. The Minoslight distorted colors, ruddy hair and long green eyes became something else, but the freckled snub nose and the wide mouth and the small square chin were more pleasing than . . . oh, than that Dyckman build, supposed to be so female. The Dyckmans were just *sloppy*. Barbara hugged her own wide shoulders, ran hands over firm young breasts, down supple flanks and legs. She wasn't too thin, she reassured herself a little anxiously. Except around the high cheekbones, she hadn't an angle which wasn't
19

properly rounded off. She shivered as the wind dried her skin, picked up her clothes and departed.

The dying hearthfire within the barrack led her to her place. She threaded a way between long-limbed forms sprawled on straw ticks, hung her harness on its peg and stowed her weapons in their chest, trying to be quiet. But Whitleys were light sleepers, and her cousin Valeria woke up.

"Oh, it's you. Two left feet as always," snarled Valeria, "and each one bigger than the other. Where did you park your fat rump all day?"

Barbara looked at the face which mirrored her own. They were the only Whitleys in Freetoon, their mothers and aunts died in the Greendale ambush fifteen years ago, and they should have been as close as cousins normally were. But theirs was a trigger-tempered breed, and when a new wing leader corporal was required, the sacred dice had chosen Barbara. Valeria could not forgive that.

"I took my two left feet and my fat rump—if you *must* describe yourself that way—into the valley and captured a Monster in a star ship," said Barbara sweetly. "Good night." She lay down on her pallet and closed her eyes.

But not long. Bee had not even risen when there was a clank of metal in the doorway and Ginny Latvala of the Udall bodyguard shouted: "Up, Corporal Maiden Barbara Whitley! You're wanted at the Big House."

"Do you have to wake everyone else on that account?" snapped Valeria, but not very loud. The entire company had been roused, and Captain Kim Trevor was a martinet.

Barbara got to her feet, feeling her heart knock. Yesterday seemed somehow unreal, like a wild dream . . .

Ginny leaned on her spear, waiting. "The Old Udall is pretty mad at you, dear," she confided. "We may have all sorts of trouble coming because you roped that Monster. Suppose it gets angry? Suppose it has friends?" The Latvalas were slim blonde girls, handy with a javelin and so made hereditary guards in most towns. They were pleasant enough, but inclined to snobbishness.

"I have my rights," said Barbara huffily. "All the scouts got their orders before witnesses, and I was never ordered *not* to lasso a Monster."

She let the barrack buzz around her while she dressed

20

for the occasion: a short white skirt, an embroidered green cloak, sandals, and dagger. Nobody outside the Big House, except the few troopers she had met who helped her bring the Monster home, knew what had happened. Yet! Barbara and Ginny agreed silently that it would be good for their souls to wonder a while.

The air was still cold and the fields below the town white with mist when she came out. A pale rosy light lifted above the eastern Ridge, and Minos was waning. The moon Theseus was a wan red sickle caught in the sunrise.

There were not many people up. A patrol tramped past Barbara and Ginny in full harness, all of them husky Macklins, and the farmhand caste yawned out of their barracks on the way to a day's hoeing. The street climbed steeply upward from the cavalry house, and Barbara took it with a mountaineer's long slow stride, too worried to heed Ginny's chatter. They went past the weavery; she glimpsed looms and spinning wheels within the door, but it didn't register on her mind—low-caste work. The smithy, a highly respected shop, lay beyond, also empty; the Holloways still slept in their adjoining home.

Sickbay was not on this street, but the maternity hospital was, on the other side of the broad plaza. Hard by it were the nurseries. Both stood just under the walls of the Big House, so the children could be moved into its shelter first in case of attack.

Passing the shuttered window of one of the rooms into which the nurseries were divided, Barbara heard a small wail. It grew, angrily, and then stopped.

The sound broke through her worry with an odd little tug at her soul. In another year or so, she would be an initiate, and make the journey to the Ship. And when she came back, no longer called Maiden, there would be another redhaired Whitley beneath her heart. Babies were a nuisance, in a way; she'd have to stay within town till hers was weaned, and—and—it was hard to wait.

The stockade bulked above her, great sharp stakes lashed together and six Latvalas on guard at the gate. They dipped their spears and Barbara went through.

Inside, there was a broad cobbled yard with several buildings neatly arrayed: barracks, stables, storehouses, emergency shelters, the Father chapel. All were in the normal Freetoon style, long log houses with peaked sod roofs and a fireplace at one end. The hall, in the middle, was much the same, but immensely bigger, its beam ends carved into birds of prey.

Henrietta Udall stood at its door. She was the oldest of Claudia's three daughters: big and blocky, with harsh black hair, small pale eyes under tufted brows. The finery of embroidered skirt and feather cloak was wasted on her, Barbara thought, and the axe she carried didn't help matters much. None of the Udalls could ever be handsome. But they could lead!

"Halt!"

Barbara came to a stop, spread her hands and lowered her head.

"Your hair is a mess," said Henrietta. "Do those braids over."

"But your mother wants to see me now," protested Barbara.

Henrietta hefted her axe. Ginny looked uneasy. "You heard me."

Barbara bit her lip and began uncoiling the bronze mane. It was hacked off just below her shoulders.

Spiteful blowhard, she thought. *Wants to get me in trouble. Come the day, Henrietta, and you won't find me on your side.*

The death of an Udall was always the signal for turmoil. Theoretically, the power went to her oldest daughter. In practice, the sisters were as likely as not to fight it out between themselves; a defeated survivor fled into the wilderness with her followers and tried to start a new settlement. Freetoon was old, almost a hundred years, and had already begotten Newburh. Now the population was up again to nearly eight thousand, about as many as the arable land within a safe distance could support.

Daydreams of heading into unknown country for a fresh start drove the sulkiness from Barbara. If, say, she rose high in the favor of Gertrude or Anne . . . she might become more than a noncom, and her daughters would inherit the higher caste, and . . .

"Hurry it up! The Old Udall is waiting."

Barbara used some choice cavalry language under her breath. The chance of reaching her dream was very little,

22

after all. Whitleys just weren't politicians. It wasn't worth it.

"All right," said Henrietta as Bee rose. She led the way inside. Barbara followed, her face still hot.

The main room of the Big House was long, and despite the fire and the opened windows and the bright tapestries it was gloomy. Sconced torches guttered above the Old Udall's seat, and the conifer boughs strewn on the dirt floor rustled as Barbara walked over them. Servants scurried around, ignored by the middle-aged, high-caste women seated on the bench below the throne. They were having breakfast, gnawing the drumsticks of runners and tossing the bones to the aquils which swooped from the rafters.

"Well!" said Claudia. "It took you long enough."

Barbara had learned the hard way never to blame an Udall for anything. "I'm sorry, ma'am," she muttered. It was an effort to get the words out and to bend the knee.

The Old Udall finished a bone and snapped her fingers. While an adolescent Craig ran up with a wooden plate of choice pieces, she leaned back and let her chambermaid comb the stiff gray hair.

Elinor Dyckman had gotten that job. The Dyckmans were good at flattery. There weren't many of them in any town; they had small mother instinct and neglected their children, so that the youngsters often died. But they were said to be shrewd advisers. Certainly they did well enough for themselves. A Dyckman nearly always became the lover of someone influential; Elinor had latched onto Claudia herself. Barbara's scornful reflection, *I wouldn't be a parasite like that,* was tinged with wistfulness. No Whitley ever had a sweetheart. Their breed was too independent and uncompromising—or too huffy, if you wanted a more common description of them.

Elinor was in her middle twenties; her own baby was dead and she hadn't asked for another. She was medium tall, with a soft curving body and soft bluish-black hair. Her small heart-shaped face smiled sweetly on the chief, and she combed with long slow strokes.

"You'll have to be punished for that," said the Old Udall. "Suggestions, Elinor dear?" She laughed.

Elinor blinked incredible lashes over melting dark eyes

23

and said: "Not too severe, ma'am. Babs means well. A little KP ought to . . ."

Barbara's hand fell to her dagger. "I'm in the army, you milk-livered trull!"

"Watch your language," said the Counselor Marian Burke, white-haired and rheumatic.

Barbara stamped her foot. Since she wasn't wearing boots, it hurt, and tears stung her eyes. "Ma'am, you know the law," she said thickly. "If I'm to be so disgraced—*dishwashing, by Father!*—I demand a court-martial."

"You'll demand nothing!" snapped Claudia.

Elinor smiled and went on combing. "It was only a joke," she murmured. "Hadn't we better get down to business?"

The Old Udall gazed at Barbara. *Trying to stare me down, are you?* thought the girl savagely. She would not look away. There was a silence that stretched.

Then an aquil stooped, to snatch a piece of meat off the table, and the serving girls screamed indignantly. Claudia chuckled. "Enough," she said. "Yes, Elinor, you're right as usual, we can't stop to quarrel now."

She leaned ponderously forward. "I've heard reports from the scouts," she went on. "Most of them, of course, saw nothing, and returned by nightfall. There were about half a dozen in your vicinity who saw you and helped you bring the Monster back. Their ranking officer has told me what you did."

Barbara remained silent, not trusting her tongue. Captain Janet Lundgard had emerged from the woods and taken charge: set a guard on the ship, slung the unconscious Monster on a spare orsper, and ridden to town with the rest of them for escort. She had reported directly to the Big House while the others went back to barracks. But what had she told?

"Apparently you attacked the Monster unprovoked," said Claudia Udall coldly. "Father knows what revenge it may take."

"It had drawn a weapon on me, Ma'am," answered Barbara. "If I hadn't lassoed it, maybe it would have destroyed all Freetoon. As it is, we have the thing a prisoner now, don't we?"

24

"It may have friends," whispered Elinor, her eyes very large. A shiver went through the hall.

"Then we have a hostage," snapped Barbara.

The Old Udall nodded. "Yes . . . there is that. I've had relays of guards sent to its ship. None of them report any sign of life. It, the Monster, must have been alone."

"How many other ships have landed, all over Atlantis?" wondered Henrietta.

"That's what we have to find out," said Claudia. You had to admit the Udalls were brave enough; they faced a situation and made a swift decision and stuck by it. "I'm sending a party to the Ship—the Ship of Father—to ask the Doctors about this. We'll also have to send scouts to the nearest other towns, find out if they've been visited too."

Both missions would be dangerous enough. Barbara thought with a tingling what her punishment would be. As a non-initiate, she couldn't go to the Ship, but she would be sent on a mission toward Greendale, Highbridge, or Blockhouse, to spy. *But that's terrific! When do we start?*

The Udall smiled grimly. "And meanwhile, for weeks perhaps, we'll have the Monster to deal with . . . and our own people. This can't be hushed up. The whole town must already be getting into a panic.

"We have to learn the truth about the Monster . . . yes, and all the people had better know the facts. We'll do it this way. The carpenters will set up a cage for the Monster, right in the plaza, and while everybody not on duty watches, someone will go into that cage and we'll see what happens."

Barbara felt sweat on her skin, and there was a brief darkness before her eyes.

"Who's going to volunteer for *that* job?" grumbled Marian Burke.

Elinor smiled. "Why, who but our brave Corporal Whitley?" she answered.

CHAPTER V

Davis Bertram kept waking up. Then some new jolt would throw him back into blankness. A few times he tried to talk, but only a hoarse gobble came out. Finally everything passed over in a heavy sleep.

He came back to half consciousness in a night as thick as the taste in his mouth. A while he lay existing, a mere collection of assorted pains. Eventually it occurred to him that he might open one eye.

Straw rustled beneath him. His arms didn't respond to his will, something held them, but he got to a kneeling position. Now he could sense he was between walls. A door was vaguely outlined, yellowish light seeping past its edges. Davis stumped forward, propelled more by instinct than any decision, until he knelt against the door. He retched. Leaning his forehead against rough wood, he had an eye close to a hole. Out of some forgotten past experience, words trickled: *Hole for a latchstring.* He bleared a glance through it.

A courtyard lay under flooding amber radiance. He could see how each individual cobblestone humped up from a puddle of darkness, into that glow. On the farther side, another building was silhouetted against a purple-black sky where stars twinkled. In front of this was a, what, oh, yes, a stone trough.

He wondered dully where he was and what had happened. Then the dullness vanished.

A girl walked out of the opposite place. She was tall and lithe, clad in a rigid upper garment, short skirt, and high boots. She carried a helmet under one arm; the light seemed to strike sparks from her hair. He associated her, incoherently, with a terrible curve-beaked bird, with panic and pain. But he didn't cringe. Whatever had occurred, she made up for it now.

Stopping by the trough, she laid down her iron hat, put one foot on the edge, unlaced a boot and removed it. Then the other. Her legs were terrific. She jerked at straps and buckles, took off her corselet, wriggled from the undershirt.

Davis gasped. Her breasts stood forth from shadow, gleaming in the light, like the cobblestones: but there the resemblance ended. *Fifth order function, isn't it?* said his mathematical reflexes. *Five points of inflection, counting the central cusp as three.* He checked again to make sure. Yes, five. Of course, his mind mumbled, that was thinking in terms of plane geometry, whereas the view here was decidedly three-dimensional. . . . . The girl stretched herself, muscle by muscle, standing on tiptoe and arching her back. *Four-dimensional! Mustn't forget the time variable!*

She undid her belt, stepped out of kilt and undergarment. *Yow!* thought Davis. He would have spoken it if his mouth hadn't been so puffy; he was stiff and swollen in a number of places.

The girl scooped handfuls of water from the trough and washed herself. The clear splashings were the only sound in all the night. Afterward she unbraided her hair and shook it loose down her back. A small breeze played with her locks and slid about her body. Davis wished he were a small breeze. Drops of water sparkled on her skin, wherever shadows did not edge roundedness. She leaned over the trough, stared into it, touched herself and smiled. It made her look very young. Not too young, though. She shivered, which was also a sight worth watching, gathered her stuff and walked out of sight.

Davis lay down on the straw again. His battered self was still not functioning very well. The vision felt like a dream, already fading in his mind. But a most consolatory dream. . . . . *Delirium,* he decided as the hormones stopped moaning. *All quite impossible. Too bad.* He plunged back into unconsciousness.

He woke when the door was opened and lay there for a minute, trying to remember where he was and what had happened and why his flesh ached in a hundred places. After two short-lived attempts, he got his eyes to function.

27

There was a spurred boot in front of his nose. He rolled over, cautiously, letting his gaze travel upward. The boot, a laced affair of reddish leather, ended at a shapely knee. Above was a kilt of leather strips with iron bands clinched on as reinforcement. There was a wide belt supporting a sheathed knife on one side and a small pouch on the other. The belt went over a laminated cuirass of hardened leather, breastplate and backplate laced around a slender torso; a bust bucket of thin iron jutted from the front. Then there was a slim neck, a lot of yellow hair braided under a flat helmet with plumes, and a rather attractive sun-tanned face.

Davis sat up, remembering. Cosmos! That girl on the nightmare bird, the lariat and . . .

"What's going on?" he croaked. "Who are you?"

"F-Father!" stammered one of the girls. "It talks!"

She spoke Basic—a slurred, archaic form, but it was the Basic of Earth and all human planets. She must be human, thought Davis weakly; no alien was that humanoid.

A handsome wench, too, though a bit muscular for his taste. Davis began to smile through bruised lips at all ten of them.

"Gak!" he said.

The ten were identical.

Well, not quite . . . some leaned on spears and some bore light, wicked-looking axes, and some had a beltful of needle-nosed darts. That was not an enjoyable way of distinguishing girls.

He shuddered and grew aware that he had been stripped. He scrambled to his feet. Now Davis' home planet was a trifle on the cold side, and its customs had developed accordingly. They didn't exactly include a nudity taboo, but he had certainly found summer days on Earth—with too intellectualized a culture for taboos of any sort—more than a little distracting. "Sunblaze!" he gulped, under the interested eyes of decuplet girls. A jerk at the wrists told him his hands were tied behind his back. He sat down again, lifting his knees and glaring across them.

"I imagine Monsters would have learned the Men language, Ginny," said one of his visitors. On closer ob-

28

servation, Davis saw that she was older—in fact, the ages seemed to range from twenty to forty—and had a scar on one cheek. Some kind of insigne was painted on her breastplate—sunblaze, it was the six-pointed star of an astrogator's mate!

"It *looks* harmless," said one of the younger women doubtfully.

"Let's get it out, then," decided the officer. "You, Monster!" She shouted at him, as if to help him understand. "We friends. We not hurt-um you. You obey-um. Or else you get-um spear in-um guts."

"But *I'm* a friend too!" wailed Davis.

"Up!" said the officer, raising her battle-axe. She was tense as a drawn wire—they all were, all more than half afraid of him and doubly dangerous on that account. Davis rose.

They formed a circle and marched him out of the shed. He saw a courtyard, rudely paved with stones, a number of primitive buildings, and a high palisade around all. There was a catwalk beneath the stakes, and warriors posted on it with some kind of crossbow.

When he came out of the gate, Davis saw quite a small army alert for whatever he might try. Some were on foot, some mounted on birds like the one he'd seen before: larger and stouter than ostriches, with feathers of blue-tipped white and cruel hawk heads. He decided not to try anything.

A rutted unpaved street snaked downhill between big, clumsy houses. Beyond the town, it became a road of sorts, wandering through cultivated grainfields; he could just see the forms of laborers out there, guarded by a few girls on birdback. The fields covered a sloping, boulder-strewn plateau, which dipped off into the forest and ran down toward the remote river valley. Behind the castle, the mountains rose steep and wooded.

Ignoring botanical details, this might also have been Earth of some older age. But not when you looked at the sky. It was a terrestrial heaven, yes, blue and clear, with towering white cumulus masses in the west. Overhead, though, were two crescent moons, dim by daylight, one almost twice the apparent size of Earth's, the other half again as big as Luna seen from home. And there was the emperor planet, the world of which *this* was only another satellite. When full, it would sprawl across fourteen times as much sky as Luna. Just now it was a narrow sickle, pale amber. The morning sun was approaching it. That is, the smaller, Sol-type sun, Delta Capitis Lupi B in standard astrographic language, about which the giant planet moved. The primary sun, bluish-white A, had not yet risen; it would never seem more than the brightest of the stars.

Davis shook an aching head and wrenched his attention back to the ground. Be damned if this was like Earth, after all, even with the women and children clustered around and chattering. Not just their dress—the cilivians wore little, the kids nothing. Their *likeness*. Women and children—all female, the children—seemed to be cast from a few hundred molds. Take two from the same mold, like those gawping dairymaid types over there, and the only difference was age and scars.

Cosmos, but he was thirsty!

The procession debouched on a wide open space. At its farther end were some thousands of civilians, jammed together, craning their necks, held back by a line of guards. Their high-pitched, excited voices sawed on his nerves. In the middle of the square was a tall old tree, not unlike an elm if you didn't look too closely, and beneath this was a large wooden cage.

"In there," said the blonde captain. She drew her knife and cut his bonds.

Davis shuffled through the cage door. "Is this a zoo?" he asked. "Where are all the men, anyway?"

"Don't *you* know?" The captain almost dropped her knife.

"Look here—I—oh, never mind!"

"Very well, Babs, let's see how you get out of this one!"

It was a new voice, quite low and attractive. Davis looked through the bars and saw a redhaired girl among the cavalry—the same one who'd roped him yesterday!

Or was she? Her twin, also in armor, came walking slowly forth across the square, carrying a tray. Davis stepped warily back as the newcomer entered his prison. The blonde officer shut the door on them, clicked down the

30

latch, and stood aside with a struggle between dignity and relief.

The girl put down her tray and touched her dagger. She was cute, thought Davis; he could have gone for her in better circumstances. Her greenish eyes widened, and she breathed hard.

"Will you eat, Monster?" she whispered.

Davis saw food on the tray, a roast fowl, and some kind of tuber, a bowl of yellow liquid, a dish of fruit. He hesitated, thinking about poison. Terrestroid worlds were tricky that way.

But his biotic analyzers had told him the life here was both harmless and nourishing; nor had they found any microorganisms which would regard him as a free lunch. Of course, he had only sampled one small area . . .

But *she* was human. They all were. If they could live on this stuff, so could he.

He gulped down the drink, a thin sour beer which made him wolfish for the food. He squatted down and ripped it between his teeth.

Four women came near the cage, all of the same unprepossessing genotype. The oldest wore a headdress of plumes. "Well, Corporal," she snapped, "question it."

"Yes—yes, ma'am," said the girl in a small voice. She stood as far from Davis as she could get. "I—I am Corporal Maiden Barbara Whitley, Monster."

"The one who captured you," said one of the elders.

"Be quiet, Henrietta," said the oldest. With a certain fearless price: "I am Claudia, the Udall of Freetoon."

"Honored, Citizen," said Davis between bites. "My name is Davis Bertram T." She didn't ask him about the initial, and he saw no reason to explain it stood for Terwilliger.

"Why . . . that could be a human name," said Barbara shyly.

"It is," said Davis. He was beginning to feel better, almost kindly. "What else should it be?"

"Oh—oh, yes, the stories did say you Monsters learned the arts from the Men." She smiled, the least little bit.

"But I—" Davis stood up. "Who said I was a monster?" He was not, he told himself, vain; but more

31

than one woman had informed she liked his face.

"But you are! *Look* at you!"

"Damn it, I'm not! I'm as human as you are!"

"With all that hair?" snapped Henrietta Udall.

"Let the corporal do the talking," said Claudia.

Davis fingered his chin. He'd never had a strong growth of beard, and the stubble was scarcely visible even now. He gave the Udalls an unfriendly glance. "You've got more mustache than I do," he growled.

"Look here," said Barbara reasonably. "we're not blind. I admit you're not unlike a person. You have two legs and five fingers and no feathers. But you're bigger than any of us, and haven't got any more breasts than a ten-year-old."

"I should hope not!" said Davis.

"In fact—" Barbara scratched her neck, puzzledly, and pointed. "Just what *is* that? Do you fight with it?"

"It doesn't look prehensile," said the blond captain.

If he hadn't still had a headache, Davis would have been tempted to beat his skull against the bars. He told himself wildly that he had not gone insane, that he was not delirious, that he really was here on the Earth-sized third satellite of Delta Capitis Lupi B I. But somehow it seemed to slip through his fingers.

He put his face in his palms and shuddered.

"Poor Monster." The girl trod impulsively forward and laid a hand on his arm. "You haven't been very well treated, have you?"

He looked up. She paled a little with fright, under the smooth brown skin, and made half a step back. Then her lips stiffened—unfairly attractive lips—and she stayed where she was.

"We had no way of knowing," she said. "The stories are so old and so vague. Some Monsters are friendly with the Men and some aren't. We couldn't take chances."

"But I am a man!" shouted Davis.

A groan went through the crowd. Somebody screamed.

Barbara clenched her fists. "Why did you say that?" she asked in a wobbly voice.

"Can't you *see*, girl?"

"But the Men . . . the Men are powerful, and beautiful, and—"

32

"Oh, Evil!" Davis took her fingers, they felt cold in his, and laid them against his cheek. "Feel that? I haven't got much yet in the way of whiskers, but . . ."

Barbara turned faintly toward the Udall. "It's true, ma'am," she whispered. "There's hair starting to grow out of his face."

"But you lassoed him!" said the blonde captain. "We fetched him back on an orsper like a sack of meal!"

"Yeh," cried a voice in the crowd. "If he's a Man, where's his comb and wattles?"

Davis took hold of his sanity with both hands. "Look," he began between clenched teeth. "Look, let's be reasonable about this. Just what the jumping blue blazes do you think a man is?"

"A Man is . . . is . . . a human male." He could barely hear the Barbara girl's reply.

"Good. And what is a male?"

"Don't you *know?*"

Davis drew several long breaths before answering: "Yes. I do know. I want to find out if you do."

"A male is . . . well . . . there are male animals and female animals. A male fertilizes the female and she brings forth the eggs . . . or the living young, in the case of some fish and snakes . . ."

"All right. I just wanted to get that settled. Now—have you ever seen a human male before?"

"Certainly not." Her courage was returning. "You must indeed be from far away, Monster. There are no Men on all Atlantis."

"Oh . . . is that what you've called this world? But how do you manage—how long since . . ."

"Humans came here some three hundred years ago," she said. "That is, by a year I mean the time Minos needs to go once around the sun Bee."

Minos . . . the big planet, of course. Davis had measured from space that it was about one Astronomical Unit from B, which had nearly the same mass as Sol. So one Minos year was approximately one Earth year. Three centuries—why, they were barely starting to colonize then! The hyperdrive was newly invented and . . .

"But you have children!" said Davis feebly.

"Oh, yes. By the grace of Father, the Doctors at His

33

Ship can— I don't know any more. I've never been there."

Davis took a while to swallow that one.

At least these barbarians had preserved something: a little elementary astronomy, the Basic language, the idea of farming and metallurgy. A shipwreck three hundred years ago, and an incredible hoax played by some gang known as the Doctors . . .

"Very well," he said at length. "Thanks, Barbara. Now we're getting somewhere. You see, I *am* a man, a human male."

"Nonsense!" snorted the old battle-axe in the war-bonnet.

Davis felt trapped. It was worse than being asked to prove by rigorous logic that he existed.

Something came back to him. In the few hours he'd been on Atlantis, before this Barbara wench caught him, he had seen plenty of animal life. Lizard-like forms, fish in a brook, flying birds and frightless birds. Some of the earthbound avians had been the size of buffalo.

But no mammals. In all those herds and flocks, not a mammal. And the girl had said . . .

Excitement gripped him. "Wait a minute!" he cried. "Are there any . . . well, I mean, does Atlantis harbor any warm-blooded animals with hair that give live birth and suckle their young?"

"Why, no," said Barbara. "None but us, and our folk came from the stars."

"Ahhh-*ha*. Mammals never evolved here, then. No wonder you didn't recognize—I mean, uh . . ."

"What do you mean?" asked Barbara innocently.

Davis' tongue knotted up on him. Since the mammal is the only terrestroid life form whose males—apart from all secondary characteristics—are conspicuously male, it was understandable that a certain confusion existed on Atlantis. But he didn't feel up to explaining such matters. He didn't feel up to much of anything. They probably wouldn't believe him in all events.

"This is ridiculous," barked the Old Udall. "It's well understood that the Men will come in all their power and glory. This wretch is a Monster, and the only question is what to do about it."

Another girl trod forth. Even now, Davis felt his eyes

34

bug out. She was dark, throaty-voiced, with gold bangles on slender arms and red flowers in her long black hair, high in the prow and walking like a sine wave. "Please, ma'am," she said. "I have an idea."

The Old Udall smiled at her. "Yes, Elinor?"

"It says it is a Man." Elinor waggled her lashes at Davis. "Let it prove it."

"How?" demanded Davis eagerly.

"Barbara," said Elinor with scientific detachment.

"What?"

"Certainly," said Elinor. "Just fertilize the corporal."

Barbara stepped back, white-faced. "No!" she gasped.

"Why, think of the honor, dear Babs," purred Elinor. "The first woman in three hundred years to have a child by a living Man. I think . . . don't you think, ma'am, anyone getting such an honor should be upgraded?"

"Indeed I do," said Claudia earnestly. "Corporal Whitley, we've had our little differences, but now the future of Freetoon may depend on you. You won't fail your duty."

"My duty isn't . . ."

"Or are you afraid?" murmured Elinor.

Davis saw Barbara flush red. She knotted her fists and closed her eyes. After a very long minute, she opened them again and looked squarely at him with an air of having but one life to give for her country.

"Yes," she said defiantly. "You may fertilize me, Davis—if you can!"

Davis looked at several thousand interested faces. He wished he could disappear.

How did you explain the effect of social conditioning to a tribe which had never heard of such matters?

"Not now," he begged hoarsely. "Give me time . . . privacy . . . I can't do anything *here* . . ."

The Old Udall lifted a skeptical brow.

"Oh, never mind," said Davis. "Have it your way. I'm a monster."

CHAPTER VI

Barbara was not happy.

That sorry business in the plaza had returned her to Claudia's favor and won her a good deal of respect elsewhere. After all, nobody knew if the Monster had poison fangs. Thinking back, though, she could only remember how bruised and beaten the poor creature had been. Evil or not, someone who rode proudly between the stars shouldn't be questioned before a crowd of lunkheads.

In the four days since, she had been out hunting. The great grazing birds could not be domesticated—hard enough to tame the carnivorous orspers—and the small fowl at home furnished no steaks. Her peacetime duty was to keep up Freetoon's meat and leather supply. Usually the huntresses went in groups, for help and saftey: the local game, grown timid, often had to be tracked for days. This trip Barbara elected to make alone. She found it ever harder to get along with anyone.

We Whitleys are a crotchery lot, she admitted. For once, the reflection was less arrogant than gloomy. Perhaps the sight of the lonely captive Monster had changed her viewpoint. If there were more of her family in Freetoon, it might have been different; she couldn't have quarreled with all of them, and her mother she remembered as a tall kindliness.

Childhood friends grew apart. That was the curse of the Whitleys. They had good enough minds and a proud enough tradition to be the equals of Latvalas, Trevors, Lundgards . . . but they were too short-tempered, too impolitic to belong to so high a caste. After the rites of becoming acolyte, when serious training began, a barrier grew up. In early adolescence, a Whitley nearly always got a crush on an older Trevor. But it was never reciprocated,

36

and after a few years it died away leaving its scar, and the Whitley made her own lonesome road through life.

But that Monster! Ever since she had been in the cage with it, there had been this moodiness. Had the Monster psyched her?

The vagueness of the concept was frightening. They whispered about it on winter nights, psyching, that was something the ancestresses had done, undefined, dark, and powerful. The lower castes had charms against being psyched by the Critters and the Cobblies and other unseen mountain dwellers.

To escape herself, therefore, Barbara got Kim Trevor's permission to hunt, saddled one orsper and took another to pack home her kill, and headed northward into the Ridge.

She spoored a stamper herd on the second day and caught up to it on the third. After dark, in a light rain, she shot one of them and stampeded the rest. Otherwise the old male would try to kill her. Then she had to stand guard against the jacklins that coughed and boomed in the forest, drawn by the smell of blood. Toward morning the rain stopped and the sky cleared; she set to work cutting up the bird and finished quickly.

And now the night was suddenly cool, a bright mystery where wet leaves sparkled gold beneath Minos, a scent of young blossoms, the High Gaunt rearing its stern stone peak like a lance among the stars. An irrational happiness filled her. There was a tingle all through her.

And this was not to be understood either. After a while she grew scared of it, and by dawn she was back in the blackest depression.

"I wonder what's happening to the Monster?" she said. Her voice seemed unnaturally loud in the mists. It was high time she got home. The trail had arced, so that she could be in Freetoon tonight if she cut across the Geyser Flats and rode hard. Suddenly she wanted very much the harsh sweaty comfort of the barracks.

Sleep was no problem. Normally you slept about four hours out of the twelve between a sunset and a sunset, but huntresses could go for days on birdnaps. Barbara fed her orspers, loaded the pack bird, and started back at a trot. She ate in the saddle, not stopping even for the holy time of eclipse, when Bee went behind Minos and the stars

37

came out. Ay and Ariadne gave light enough for those ten-plus minutes, and a muttered prayer to Father met minimum requirements.

Shortly afterward she struck the Ironhill road. It was wider and more rutted than most. "All roads lead to Iron-hill"—its folk supplied metals from their mines, trading for the timber of the forest people, the grain and jerked meat of the valley settlements, the salt and fish of the seadwellers. You could buy anything in Ironhill.

Otherwise there was not much trade between towns. They were too scattered and too hostile.

Jogging along in her own gloom, Barbara forgot all caution. She rounded a bend and could have been shot by the Greendalers before realizing they were there.

A dozen of them, in full armor, riding toward Freetoon . . . the standard bearer had their flag on a tall shaft, the double sun emblem, but there was the white cloth of truce a-flutter beneath it. Barbara reined in, gasping, and stared at the crossbows as they swiveled around. She wore only the doublet and kilt of the pot-hunter.

The Greendale leader laughed. "We won't harm you to-day, darling, if you behave yourself," she said. She was a middle-aged Macklin with a broken nose and some missing teeth. "Freetooner yourself, aren't you? We're going your way."

Barbara nodded distantly and joined their party. She didn't hate them, but war was as normal a part of life as the harvest festival. She had been in several raids and skirmishes since gaining her growth, and her kin were dead at Greendale hands.

There was a Whitley sergeant in the band, about fifty years old. Barbara rode beside her. "I'm Gail," she introduced herself. "I see you had luck. There hasn't been a stamper herd in our territory for fifteen years."

"What's your mission?" asked Barbara, rather snap-pishly.

"What do you think?" answered Gail. "You people ought to know better than to send spies our way when I'm on patrol duty."

"Oh. You bushwhacked them, then." Barbara felt a cold stabbing along her spine.

"Every one. Caught three of them alive. One . . . Avis

Damon, yes, that's her name . . . got pretty much cut up in the fracas, and rather than bleed to death she told us what she knew."

It was bad news—very bad—but Barbara's first reaction was scorn. "I always claimed those Damons aren't fit for combat." Then, slowly: "So what do you think you learned?"

"A star ship landed in your country." Gail said it with care, and a ghost of fear flickered in her eyes. "There was a Man aboard."

"A Monster," corrected Barbara. "We made it admit that."

"Mmmm . . . yes . . . I thought so myself. You couldn't have captured a Man against his will."

A thin, dark-haired Burke interrupted, above the plopping feet and creaking leather: "Are you sure it was against his will?"

That was the trouble with the Burkes. They thought too much, they disquieted everybody. Barbara's hands felt clammy. "Yes." she answered. "I myself dragged the Monster at a lasso's end."

"If it is a test of faith, though . . ." The Burke shook her head dubiously.

"Shut up!" There was a harsh, strained note in the Macklin captain's voice. She turned around and said to Barbara: "What plans do you have now?"

"I don't know. I've been gone ever since— We've sent to the Doctors, of course, to ask what we ought to do."

"And meanwhile you have the Monster. The ship can fly, and the Monster knows how to make it fly." Anger writhed across the leathery face. "Do you think we're going to stand by and let you make an ally of the Monster?"

"What do you want?" replied Barbara.

"We're bringing an ultimatum," said Gail Whitley. "Your Udall has to turn the Monster over to a joint guard till we get word from the Ship of Father. That'll take many days, and we're not going to let you have that power all to yourselves in the meantime."

"And if we don't?" asked Barbara unnecessarily.

"War," said Gail, equally redundant.

Barbara thought about it for a while. She ought to make

a break for it, try to reach Freetoon ahead of this gang . . . no, that would earn her nothing more than a bolt in the back. There was going to be war; no Udall would cough up a prize like the Monster. The two towns were pretty evenly matched. Freetoon could not be taken by the Greendalers and the crops were too young to burn —*anyway, who says we can't defend our own fields? We'll toss them out on their rumps, and chase them all the way home.*

The battle would probably start tomorrow, the ultimatum being refused tonight. It was about thirty hours' ride to Greendale—less by the roads, but an army didn't want to be too conspicuous en route. The enemy soldiers must already have left and be bivouacked somewhere in the Ridge.

So be it! Barbara felt a welcome tension, almost an eagerness. It was a pleasant change from her mood of the past days.

The Burke girl took a small harp from her saddlebag, and the band broke into song, one of the good old stirring cavalry songs said to go back to the Men themselves . . . Barbara chimed in, the orspers broke into a brisk jog, and they all enjoyed the rest of the trip.

Bee and Ay were under the horizon when they clattered up to Freetoon, but Minos, Ariadne, Theseus, and the two tiny moons Aegeus and Pirithous gave plenty of light. The outer patrols stopped them on the edge of the grainfields and then, not daring to leave the post when an army might be near, sent them on in Barbara's charge.

The embassy had dismounted in the courtyard and stamped into the Big House when Barbara realized her usefulness was over. She turned her kill over to the servants and put the two orspers in the castle barn. Poor birds, they were so tired. Then she wondered what to do. Go back to barracks, where the girls sat around the hearth talking, drinking, playing games . . . go back and tell them what to expect? She ought to, but didn't feel like it; they'd get the word soon enough. And if there was to be combat tomorrow, she ought to have a good night's sleep, but she was too nervous.

"Where's the Monster being kept?" she asked, before thinking.

"In the shed under the north wall, ma'am," said the Nicholson groom. "Didn't dare have him anywhere but in a sep'rate building, they didn't, so we fixed the shed up nice and we brings him his meals and clean straw and water and all while the guards watches, and he ain't done no harm but . . ."

"*He!*" said Barbara. "Why do you call it he?"

"Why, he says he's male, ma'am, and, uh, well, he says . . ."

Barbara turned her back and walked out into the yard. No reason why the Monster shouldn't be male. They were Man and woman, the wise happy people of the stars, and doubtless Monsters, too . . . But why should the thought of this Davis creature's maleness be so odd to her, half frightening and thus resented?

She remembered that final ludicrous scene in the cage. Her ears burned with it . . . and why was that? If Davis had been a Man, it would have been an honor so great that . . . as it was, only Davis had been humiliated, trapped in his own pathetic lie. She had been afraid, indignant bewildered, all at once, and yet . . .

Damn Davis!

Barbara grew aware that she had walked around the Big House and was in its multiple shadow looking toward the Monster's prison.

A door of wooden bars had been erected for the shed. It . . . he . . . Davis stood against the bars, flooded with cool Minos-light and moonlight. He showed sharp and clear in the radiance, but it hazed him somehow with its own witchery; the hollow cheeks and flat hairy breast and bulging muscles were no longer ugly. They had given him clothes, kilt, cloak, and sandals; his hair was combed and a yellow beard was growing out on his face.

He was holding hands between the bars with a girl in a long feather cloak. Their voices drifted to Barbara —Elinor Dyckman, of all pests! Where did she get the right to talk alone with Davis?

"Oh, I really must be going, Bertie," she said. "Those awful Greendalers . . . didn't you see them come in? Claudia will be just *furious.*"

"Stick around, beautiful." The Monster's low chuckle was somehow paralyzing, Barbara could not have moved

41

after hearing it. "It's worth being lassoed and kicked around and caged and goggled at, just to get you here alone at last."

"Really . . . Bertie, let go of me—you scare me," Elinor tittered.

"Aw, now, I'm not going to eat you. Let me only feast on your silken hair, your starry eyes, your Cupid's-bow mouth, your swanlike throat, your . . ."

"You say *such* things." Elinor leaned closer against the door. "Nobody says such things here."

"Ah, nobody is able to appreciate you, my little one. To think I crossed the stars and found you. It was such a small deed. I ought to have moved planets, juggled suns, fought dragons to deserve a word with you. Come here . . . lend me that adorable mouth . . ."

"Bert! I . . . I . . . mmmmmm . . ."

The night blurred before Barbara. She wondered why, gulped, realized it was tears, and cursed herself.

"I *mustn't,* Bertie, dear! Claudia will be so angry. You're a . . ."

"A man. And you're a woman."

"But you said . . ."

"I had no choice then."

"Oh, I can't, Bertie, I just can't! You're locked in, and . . ."

"You can swipe the key, can't you? Of course you can. Here, give me another kiss."

It was too much. And a Whitley was no sneaking spy like a, a, a Dyckman. Barbara strode across the yard, jingling her spurs as noisily as possible. "What's going on here?" she yelled.

"Oh!" Elinor squealed. "Oh . . . Babs, is it? Babs, dear, I was only . . ."

"I know what you were only. Get out, you witch, before I knock your teeth down your throat!"

Elinor wailed and fled.

Barbara turned furiously on Davis. "What were you plotting?"

The Monster sighed, shrugged, and gave her a rueful grin. "Nothing very evil," he said. "You again, eh? It seems you always interrupt me when things are getting interesting."

Heat and cold chased each other across Barbara's face. "Maybe Father did pick me for that job," she spat. "Somebody has to keep Atlantis for the Men . . . not for your sort!"

"You know," answered Davis. "this is the kind of thing I used to daydream about in my teens. A brand new world, like Earth but more beautiful, and I the only man among a million women. Well . . . I've found it now and I want out!"

Barbara raised a fist. "Yes, so you can go home and call your friends to come raiding."

"We intend no such thing," said Davis earnestly. "We want to help you—blast it all, we're not your kind of bloodthirsty pirate. And I *am* a man, as human as you are. If you'd not come along, Elinor Dyckman would have found that out."

"Elinor!" sneered Barbara.

"All right," said Davis blandly. His smile grew altogether insolent. "Maybe you'd like to give me another chance? Honestly, you're one of the best-looking girls I've seen anywhere."

"Blast if I do!" Barbara turned her back.

"Don't go away," begged Davis. "It's lonesome as space here. All I've done is argue with that barrel-shaped queen of yours."

Barbara couldn't help it. The epithet was too good. She began to laugh and was unable to stop for a full minute.

"That's better," said Davis. "Shall we be friends?" He stuck his hand through the bars. Barbara stared at it, looked at him, he raised a mocking brow, and she gave the hand a quick clasp. She'd show him she wasn't afraid!

"Why do you claim to be a Man?" she asked. "You've already admitted that you aren't."

"I told you I had no choice then. I tell Siz Claudia that I'm a benevolent Monster and if they'll let me at my ship—under guard, if they want—I'll go home and bring the Men. I mean it, too."

"But she doesn't dare," said Barbara slowly.

"Well, not so far. Can't say I blame her. How can she know what powers I might get, once aboard my boat, and what I might do? Say have you found my blaster?"

"Your what?"

43

"My weapon. I had it in a hip holster, dropped it when you . . . No? I suppose it must be lying out in the grass somewhere. You won't find anything very useful in my pack. Medical kit, lighter, camera, a few such gadgets. I've offered to demonstrate them, but the old sow won't let me. How long am I supposed to rot here anyway?" finished Davis on a querulous note.

"What were you doing when I . . . found you?" asked Barbara.

"Just looking around. I analyzed basic surface conditions from space, then came down to let my robots check on the biochemistry and ecology. That looked safe too, so I violated all doctrine and went for a stroll. I was just coming back to the boat when— Oh, Evil, I don't imagine you understand a word." Davis smiled. "Poor kid. Poor little amazon."

"I can take care of myself!" she flared.

"No doubt. But come over here. I won't hurt you."

Barbara went to the door. He held her hands and pressed his face against the bars. "I want to show you something," he said gravely. "Maybe that way . . . one kiss, Barbara."

She couldn't help it, she felt bonelessly weak and leaned toward him.

The main door of the Big House crashed open. Torchlight flared, spilling on the cobbles, Minos became suddenly wan. Iron clanked, and the Greendale Macklin strode forth, tall and angry, her women bristling about her.

The voice jerked Barbara to awareness. She sprang from the Monster and grabbed for the crossbow at her shoulder.

"This means war!"

44

CHAPTER VII

Civilians and movable goods were brought inside the stockade that night, and armed females streamed forth. But the fighting didn't start till well after sunrise.

Davis could just hear the horns and shouts and clash of metal. There was a good-sized battle on the edge of the forest, he guessed. He looked across a courtyard littered with women, children, and assorted dry goods and wondered what the desolation to do.

Claudia Udall tramped over to his jail in full armor and toting a battle-axe. Elinor Dyckman undulated in her wake, thinly clad and scared. Davis would rather have looked at her, but thought it more tactful to meet the queen's eyes.

"Well, Monster, now a war has started on your account," said Claudia grimly.

Davis gave her a weak smile. "It wasn't my idea . . . uh, ma'am. What do they want me for, anyway?"

"The power, of course! Any town which had you and your ship could conquer the rest in days." After an embarrassing silence: "Well?"

"Well," stuttered Davis, "I offered to . . . it's too late now, isn't it? I mean, with an army between us and the boat?"

Claudia snorted. "Oh, that! We'll have those Greendale pests chased away by eclipse. But then will you help us?"

Davis hesitated. Union law was unreasonably strict about one's relationship with primitives. You could fight in self-defense, but using atomic guns to help a local aggression meant a stiff sentence.

"Let me aboard my ship . . ." he began.

"Of course," beamed Claudia. "Under guard."

"Hm, yeh, that's what I was afraid of." Davis had intended only to light out for Nerthus and never come back. Let the Service disentangle this Atlantean mess; they got paid for it. He gulped and shook his head. "Sorry, I can't. You see, uh, well, I have to be alone to make the ship work. There are rites and, uh . . . ."

"Bertie!" Elinor wobbled toward him. Her white indoor face was beaded with sweat. "Bertie, darling, you've got to help us. It's death for me if the Greendalers take this place."

"Hm?"

"Yes," she chattered frantically. "Don't you understand? The Greendale Udall already has two Dyckman attendants. They won't want a third . . . they'll see to it . . . *Ber-r-rtie!*"

Davis licked his lips. It was understandable. A queen's favorite dropped the word, and in the course of the fracas Elinor would accidentally get her throat cut. The fact that, on the winning side, she would do identically the same, was no comfort.

"Nonsense, child." Claudia glared jealously at them both. "They can't take Freetoon. There are no more of them than there are of us, and we're on home ground."

"But . . . ."

"Shut up! Monster, right now the Greendalers do hold the area where your ship is. Can they get in?"

Davis laughed nervously. "Axes and crowbars against inert steel? I'd like to see them try!"

Short of atomic tools, there was only one way to open that airlock. He had set it to respond to himself whistling a few bars of a certain ballad.

"You won't help us after we've driven them away?" Claudia narrowed her eyes.

Davis began a long speech about friends who would avenge any harm done to him. He was just getting to the section on gunboats when Claudia snorted and walked off. Elinor followed, throwing imploring looks across her shoulder.

Davis sat down on the straw and groaned. As if he didn't have troubles enough, that minx had to slither around in a thin skirt and a few beads . . . just out of reach.

Then he found himself wondering about Barbara

46

Whitley. He hoped very much she wouldn't be hurt.

Eclipse came. It happened daily, at noon in this longitude, when Atlantis, eternally facing her primary, got Minos between B and herself. An impressive sight: the planet, dimly lit by the remote companion sun, fourteen times as wide as Earth's moon, brimmed with fiery light refracted through the dense atmosphere . . . dusk on the ground and night in the sky. Davis looked hungrily at the stars. Civilized, urbane, *pleasant* stars.

The Old Udall's estimate had not been far wrong. An hour later, the battle had ended and the Freetoon girls came back to the castle. Davis noticed that the warriors were divided into about thirty genotypes, no more. When everyone in a single line of descent was genetically identical, a caste system was a natural development. And, yes, he could see why the Atlanteans had reverted to the old custom of putting surnames last. Family in the normal sense just wasn't very important here; it couldn't be.

The armored girls, foot and orsper (horse bird?) troops, clamored for lunch and beer. They had a number of prisoners; Davis saw one angry woman who was an older version of Barbara. She went haughtily toward the detention shed, ignoring a slash on her leg. Very nice looking in spite of those gray streaks in her hair; Barbara, then, would always be a handsome lass. If she was still alive. Davis watched the Freetoon casualties. There weren't many dead or seriously wounded—couldn't be, with these clumsy weapons powered by female muscles. But there had been some killed, by axe, knife, dart, bolt
. . .

"Barbara!" Davis whooped it forth.

The tall redhead looked his way and strolled through the crowd. Her left hand was wrapped in a wet crimson bandage. "Barbara! Cosmos, I'm glad you're . . ."

She gave him an unfriendly grin. "Mistake, Monster. I'm her cousin Valeria."

"Oh. Well, how is she?"

The girl shrugged. "All right. No damage. She's helping mount guard on your ship."

"Oh, then you did win."

"For now. We beat them back into the woods, but they haven't quit." Valeria gave him a hard green stare. "Now

I know you're a Monster. The Men would fight."

"Big fat chance you've given me," said Davis. "Anyway, I didn't ask for this to happen. Why can't you tribes compromise?"

"Who ever heard of an Udall compromising?" laughed Valeria.

"Then why do you obey them?"

"Why? Why, they're . . . they're the *Udalls!*" Valeria was shocked. "When I took arms, I swore . . ."

"Why did you swear? My people have learned better than to allow absolute rulers. You've got a whole world here. What is there to fight about?"

"Land, hunting grounds, honor, loot . . ."

"There's plenty of land if you wanted to move somewhere else."

"A gutless Monster *would* say that." Valeria walked away.

Davis slumped. After all, he reflected, the human race was not famous for reasonableness, and the least-effort law was hard to beat. Once the towns had gotten into the habit of obeying these Udalls . . .

The day dragged. The civilians avoided him, superstitiously, and the soldiers appeared to have other business on hand, resting, reorganizing, changing the guard. He was fed, otherwise ignored. Night came, and he tried to sleep, but there was too much noise.

Toward morning he fell into a doze, huddled under his feather quilts against the upland chill. A racket of trumpets and hurrying feet woke him.

Another battle! He strained against the bars, into darkness, wondering why this one should be so much louder. And wasn't it getting close? The sentries on the catwalk were shooting and . . .

Elinor screamed her way across the courtyard. The multiple shadows thrown by Minos and the moons rippled weirdly before her. "Bertie, you've got to help! They're driving us back!"

He reached out and patted her in a not very brotherly fashion. "There, there. There, there." When it made her hysterics worse, he shouted. After a struggle, he got some facts.

The Greendalers had returned with allies. Outnumbered

48

three to one, the Freetooners were driven back through their own streets.

Newburh, Blockhouse, and Highbridge banners flew beyond the walls. It was clear enough to Davis. Having learned about the spaceship, and well aware she couldn't take it alone, the Greendale Udall had sent off for help— days ago, probably. And the prize looked great enough to unite even these factions for a little while.

"But now Claudia will have to make terms," he blurted.

"It's too late!" sobbed Elinor. "Can't you see, now that they finally have gotten together, they'll finish us off, divide our land between them . . . Bertie, help! Help! Uhhhhh . . ."

"Let me out of here first," snapped Davis. He rattled the awkward padlock. "I can't . . . ulp!"

"What?"

"Skip it." Davis had suddenly realized there was no point in exposing himself to those crossbow quarrels which fell so nastily in the yard. The victorious allies wouldn't kill *him* if he kept safely neutral. He might even make a better deal with them.

Elinor moaned and ran toward the Big House. Only warriors were to be seen, the others had retreated into their long shed.

The fighting didn't halt even for eclipse. At midafternoon the gates opened and Freetoon's surviving soldiers poured into the court.

Step by step, the rearguard followed. Davis saw Barbara at the end of the line. She had a round wooden shield on one arm and swung a light long-shafted axe. A red lock fell from under the battered morion and plastered itself to a small, drawn face.

A burly warrior pushed against her. Barbara lifted her shield and caught the descending axe-blow on it. Her own weapon rang on the enemy's helmet, chopped for the neck, missed, and bit at the leather cuirass. It didn't go through; low-carbon steel got blunted fast. The enemy grinned and began hailing blows. Barbara sprang back. The other woman followed. Barbara threw her axe between the enemy's legs. Down went the woman. Barbara's dagger jumped into her hand; she fell on top of the other and made a deft slicing motion.

49

Davis' stomach groaned; he turned from the sight.

When he came back to the door, there was a lull in the battle. The Freetooners had been pumping bolts and javelins from the catwalk, discouraging the allies' advance long enough for the gates to be closed. There was a kind of ordered chaos, the dead and wounded dragged off, the hale springing up on the wall, fires kindled and kettles of water set over them. Davis could hear angry feminine screeches.

Presently Barbara herself came to him. She was a-shiver with weariness, and the eyes regarding him had dark rims beneath. There was blood splashed on her breastplate and arms.

"How is it for you?" she asked hoarsely.

"I'm all right." With more anxiety than a neutral party ought to feel: "Are you hurt?"

"No. But I'm afraid this is the end. We can't stand a long siege. It's early in the year, our stores are low."

"What . . . what do you think will happen? To you, I mean?"

"I'll get away at the last if I can." Her voice was numb.

Davis told himself sternly that this mess wasn't his fault. He had come to bring the gift of Union civilization. The last thing he wanted was . . .

The *first* thing he wanted, he thought, had been the glory of finding a new inhabited planet. And the money prizes, and the lucrative survey commissions, and the adoring women.

But it wasn't his doing that the woman stood mute, with red hands and bent neck, waiting to be killed.

"Cosmos curse it," he shouted, "I can't help your stupidity!"

Barbara gave him a blind, dazed look and wandered off.

The battle resumed. The invaders had cut down young trees to make scaling ladders, and there was brisk fighting on the wall. Fires roared beneath the great kettles, but that particular form of pest repellant was slow to heat up.

By Bee-set the enemy had given up the attempt, and there was a respite for eating and napping. Davis, who had always cherished a certain romantic affection for the old barbarian days on Earth, decided that if this was a fair sample there had been nothing glamorous about them—just people who hacked and shot at each other.

Claudia Udall passed as Ay went under the horizon. She stopped to give him a bleak word. "Are you ready to help us now?"

"How can I fight?" asked Davis reasonably. "I haven't got any of my weapons here. But if you'll let me out and give me the stuff from my packsack, I could do something for the wounded."

The queen cursed him, expertly, and added: "If *we* can't have you, Monster . . . I might decide not to let anybody have you."

"Yipe!" said Davis, backing away.

"Just a minute while I get a crossbow," said the Udall, and left him.

"Eek!" yelped Davis. "Hey! Come back! I'll help you!"

A fresh ruckus broke loose beyond the walls. Trumpets howled, and the resting soldiers leaped from the ground. By Minos-light Davis saw Claudia hurry toward the gate.

Thunder crashed, and the wood groaned. The ladies from Greendale must be using a battering ram. They could have cut down a big tree, put some kind of roof over it, attacked with ladders at other points to draw off the defenders . . .

Fire kindled outside; flame ran up and splashed the sky. Somehow a house must have been touched off. The top of the stockade loomed black across the blaze; like a row of teeth, the warriors on the catwalk were silhouetted devils. Davis wondered crazily which of them was Barbara, if Barbara was still alive.

The main gate shuddered and a hinge pulled loose. Freetooners jumped off the wall to make a forlorn line. There was a boilershop din of axes where the enemy came up their ladders. The fire roared, higher and higher till red light wavered over the yard.

Someone galloped toward him on a frantic orsper. She was leading two others. She jumped from the saddle and stood before the shed with an axe in her hand.

"Barbara!" he whispered.

"Valeria again." The girl laughed with scant humor. "Stand aside, I'm going to get you out."

Her axe thudded against the bolt.

"But what—why . . ."

"We're finished," snapped Valeria. "For now, anyway. For always, unless you can help us. I'm going to get you out, Monster. We'll escape if we can, and see what you can do to remedy matters."

"But I'm neutral!"

Valeria grinned unpleasantly. "I have an axe and a knife, my dear, and nothing to lose. Are you still neutral?"

"No, not if you feel that way about it."

Valeria hewed. Behind her, the gate came down and the invaders threw themselves at the defensive line.

Another orsper ran from the stables, with a rider who had a spare mount. Valeria turned, lifted her axe, lowered it again. "Oh, you."

"Same idea, I see," answered Barbara. *Of course,* thought Davis, *genetic twins normally think alike.*

"Put on your cloak, Monster," ordered Valeria between blows. "Pull the hood up. They won't bother with three people trying to get away . . . unless they know what you are!"

There was confused battle around the gate. A band of invaders had cleared a space on the catwalk, now they were leaping down to attack the Freetooners from behind.

The bolt gave way. Valeria wrenched off the lock and threw the door open. Davis stumbled out.

"Up in the saddle, you!" Valeria waved her axe at his head.

Davis got a foot in a stirrup and swung himself aboard. Valeria mounted another bird at his side; Barbara took the lead. They jogged toward the broken gate, where Claudia and a few guards still smote ferociously at a ring of enemies. The orsper's pace was not so smooth as a horse's, and Davis was painfully reminded that a mounted man does well to wear tight pants. This silly kilt was no help. He swore and stood up in the stirrups.

Someone ran from the Big House, her scream trailing. "Help Ohhhh . . ." Davis glimpsed Elinor's face, wild with terror. He leaned over, caught her wrist, whirled her toward a spare orsper.

"Get that sissy out of here!" yelled Valeria.

Elinor scrambled up. Barbara freed her axe and broke into a gallop. Willy-nilly, Davis followed.

A band of women stood before them. A bolt hummed maliciously past his ear. Barbara's orsper kicked with a gruesomely clawed foot. Valeria leaned over and swung expertly at a shadowy form; sparks showered.

Then they were past the melee, out in the street, into the fields and the forest beyond.

CHAPTER VIII

By morning they were so far into the mountains that it looked safe to rest. Davis almost fell off his orsper into the grass.

He woke up after eclipse. For a moment he knew only one pulsing ache, all over, then memory came back and he gasped.

"Are you all right?" asked Barbara.

"I'm not sure. Oof!" Davis sat up. Someone had opened a bedroll for him and gotten his snoring body into it. His legs were so sore from standing as he rode that he didn't think he would ever walk again.

"Where are we?" he inquired blearily.

"We headed north through the Ridge." Barbara pointed to a great thin peak, misty across a forested gulch. "That's the High Gaunt, so we must have come about forty kilometers. We'll eat soon."

The saddlebags held a pretty complete camping outfit. She had made a little smokeless fire and was toasting strips of dried meat. A loaf of coarse black bread and a hunk of lard lay nearby. There was a spring that burbled from rocks green with pseudomoss; Davis crawled to it and drank deep.

Then he felt well enough to look around. This was tall country, ancient woods on steep hillsides. Northward it became higher still; he could see snow on not-so-distant ranges and the ashen slopes of a volcano. The day was clear and windy; sunlight spilled across green flowery slopes and Minos brooded remotely overhead, topped by a crescent moon. Ay was a searing spark to the east, daily overtaking the closer star.

Now if only those gossiping birds would respect a man's headache . . . !

"Bertie!"

Davis lurched to his feet as Elinor came from the

woods. She had woven herself a flower garland, a big thick one which teased him with glimpses, and sleeked back her long hair. She fell into his arms and kissed him.

"Bertie, you saved my life. Oh, I'm *so* grateful . . . do you know, Bertie, *I* believe you're a Man . . ."

"You might come slice your Man some bread," said Barbara acidly.

Elinor stepped back, flushing. "Have you forgotten I'm an Udall attendant?" she shrilled.

"Aren't any more Freetoon Udalls, unless one of 'em broke away like us," snapped Barbara. "Why Davis dragged as useless a hunk of fat along as you, I'll never understand. Now come help or I'll fry you for breakfast!"

Elinor turned to Davis. "Bertie, are you going to let this low-caste witch . . ."

"I'm out of this," he said prudently.

She burst into tears. Barbara got up, cuffed her, and frogmarched her toward the ire. "You work if you want to eat."

Elinor pouted and began awkwardly sawing at the loaf. Barbara looked at Davis. "Why did you bring her?" she asked slowly.

"Holy Cosmos," he protested, "she'd have been killed if . . ."

"Better women than her are dead today. Kim, Ginny, Gretchen—I don't know if they're even alive, and you have to . . . Oh, be quiet!" Barbara went back to her work.

Valeria came into sight, crossbow on her shoulder and a plump bird in one hand. "It's easily settled," she drawled. "The Dyckman beast doesn't have to come along. Leave her here."

"No!" Elinor stood up with a shriek.

"You can ride back," sneered Valeria. "Be good for you. And I daresay you'll grease somebody into giving you a safe job."

"I'll die!" screamed Elinor. "There are jacklins in these woods! I'll be killed! You can't—*Bertie!*"

"She'd better stay with us," said Davis.

"You keep out of this," snorted Valeria.

Davis blew up. "I'll be damned to Evil if I will!" he roared. "I've been pushed around long enough!"

Valeria drew her knife. Davis cocked his fists. He'd been taught the science of self-defense and the art of boxing—which are not identical. In his present mood, he'd welcome an excuse to clip that copper-topped hellion on the jaw.

Barbara pulled down her cousin's arm. "That's enough," she said coldly. "Enough out of all of you. We have to stick together. Davis, if you insist, we'll let this . . . Elinor come along till we reach some town. Now sit down and eat!"

"Yes, ma'am," said Davis meekly.

They had their brunch in a sullen silence. But the food was strengthening; it seemed to give Davis back his manhood. After all . . . well, it was a bad situation, but he was out of that filthy jail and he was the biggest, strongest human on this planet. It was time for him to start exercising some choice.

The Whitleys calmed down as fast as they'd flared up, and Elinor showed tact enough to remain inconspicuous. Davis wished very much for a cup of coffee and a cigaret, but neither being available, he opened the council. "What are your plans?" he asked.

"I don't know," said Valeria. "Last night I only thought about getting away. Now, what do you think we can do?"

"Depends." Davis tugged at his beard. It itched, but there probably wasn't a razor on all Atlantis. "Just what will happen to Freetoon? Will the invaders kill everybody?"

"Oh, no," said Barbara. "Towns have been conquered, now and then, and the winning Udall makes herself their chief. All the civilians have to do is obey a new boss and pay her their tax and labor dues. The soldier children are brought up like the winning town's . . . yes, they usually mingle the populations."

"It's the older members of the military caste who can't be trusted," added Valeria. "People like us, who've sworn service to one Udall line. Some of them will take a fresh oath . . ."

"Damons," snorted Barbara. "Burkes. Hausers."

". . . but the rest either have to be killed or driven out. Most of our girls managed to escape, I suppose. They'll live as outlaws in the woods, or drift elsewhere to take service. Some distant town which was never an enemy . . . you know."

"Why are you still loyal to your Udalls?" asked Davis. "I can't see where you ever got much benefit from them."

"We just are!" barked the Whitleys, almost simultaneously.

"All right, all right. But look—Claudia and her daughters are most likely dead now. You haven't got any chief. You're on your own."

The cousins stared at him and at each other. They had known it intellectually, but only now did the fact penetrate.

"Maybe one of them escaped," said Barbara faintly.

"Maybe. But what do you want to *do?*"

"I don't know." Valeria scowled. "Except that the powers of your ship aren't going to be used for Bess Udall of Greendale! Not after she killed barracks mates of mine."

"I thought . . ." Barbara looked at Davis. He found it hard to meet her eyes, though he didn't know why. "I thought maybe we could sneak back, get you to your ship . . ."

"Big chance of that!" he said bitterly.

"The allies are sure to fall out over the spoils," said Valeria. "If we waited a while— No, somebody's bound to win, and that ship is going to stay guarded."

"Maybe we can find allies of our own." Barbara looked at the northern ranges. "They say there are some strange peoples living beyond Smoky Pass. Nobody's been that far for, oh, generations. If we could get help . . . promise them the loot from the enemy . . ."

"Wait a minute!" Davis broke into a new sweat. He wasn't sure how Union law would judge a case like his. A surveyor caught in a violent situation was permitted to use violence himself if it would save his life or help rectify an obviously bad run of affairs; but he didn't think a Coordinator board would see eye to eye with Barbara on what constituted rectification.

"Wait!" he said quickly. "Maybe we can do it, maybe we can't." His brain whirred at a gear-jamming speed. "But-but-but . . . look here . . . wasn't there a message already sent to, uh, this holy Ship of yours?"

57

"To the Doctors? Yes," said Valeria.

"And do *you* know what the Doctors would decide?"

"No . . . no, nothing like this has ever . . ."

Regulations said: when in doubt, the surveyor should cooperate with whatever local authority existed. And these mysterious Doctors were as close to a central government as the planet had. Furthermore, they lived in this Ship . . . the original spaceship in which the ancestresses had arrived? . . . and they knew enough science to operate a parthenogenesis machine. He'd have a better chance of convincing them of the truth than anyone else.

"So since the final disposal is up to the Doctors in all events, why don't we go there?" he proposed. "We can explain it to them and get redress for Freetoon too."

"We can't!" said Valeria, quite aghast. "Barbara and I aren't full initiates. And *you*—the Ship is sacred to Father!"

Davis was still thinking rapidly. "But I'm a man," he said, "or a monster, if you insist. The law doesn't apply to me." He glanced at Elinor. "You've been there already, haven't you?" She nodded eagerly. "All right. When we reach the taboo area, you can escort me the rest of the way."

It took a great deal of wrangling. Once Davis had to roar. Being shouted down out of bigger lungs was a new and salutary experience for the Whitleys. Eventually they agreed.

"But we can't go through the valley," said Barbara. "The Holy River highway will be guarded. You realize, Davis, there's a hunt on for you already, through the whole Ridge."

Davis gulped.

"We'll swing north," decided Valeria. "Over Smoky Pass and down through the valleys on the other side to the coast. Then we can perhaps get passage with one of the seadweller ships." Her eyes gleamed. "Quite likely the Doctors will order your boat returned to you. But as for Freetoon, they never mix in wars or politics. So if, on the way, we can make a deal with someone . . ."

"Hey!" croaked Davis.

Valeria took a whetstone from her pouch and began

honing her axe. It didn't seem worthwhile to argue further. Not just now.

"*Are* there people beyond the mountains?" asked Elinor timidly.

Davis nodded. "There must be. I could see from space, through the telescopes, that there was cultivation all over this part of the continent."

How many amazon towns were there in all—how many people? He could only guess. Let's see, about five hundred prototypes, and three hundred years in which to increase their numbers . . . less the attrition of war, wild animals, and other hazards . . . a quarter million total was a fair estimate. And they couldn't all have formed societies on the pattern of this region.

That was hopeful. He could scarcely imagine a less comfortable culture than Freetoon and Greendale.

"How long will it take us, do you think?" he inquired.

Valeria shrugged. "A few weeks, if we don't meet enemies or a late blizzard."

Atlantis, riding nearly upright in the equatorial plane of her primary, did not have seasons of Earth's kind. But the orbit of Minos was highly eccentric, as you'd expect of a planet in a double-star system. This was early summer, they were still approaching Bee, but in six months the sun would be getting farther away and there would be snow on the uplands. At these latitudes, about twenty degrees north, and at this height, Davis guessed the climate would answer to, oh, say Switzerland.

There was a permanent tidal bulge, frozen rock; the gravitation of Minos, with five thousand Earth masses, had deformed the great satellite. Most of the land was therefore on the inner hemisphere, and this central continent was a labyrinth of mountains. It was going to be a rough trip.

Davis looked at the tethered orspers, ripping up their rations with hooked beaks. "Do you have any sewing equipment?"

"Of course," said Barbara. "That's right, Davis, you'll need warmer clothes to cross the mountains."

"So will I," piped Elinor. The Whitleys paid no attention.

"This is a, uh, special garment I need," said Davis.

"I'll make it for you," said Barbara eagerly. "Just let me get the measurements."

Davis' ears glowed cadmium red. "No, thanks! You wouldn't understand."

Elinor seemed to have regained a little self-confidence. "If it's going to take us that long," she said, "the Freetoon couriers will have reached the Ship well ahead of us. The Doctors will send word back . . ."

"That's all right," said Valeria. "Just so we don't fall into Greendale hands." She drew a finger across her throat.

"Must you?" said Elinor faintly.

"And you, Davis Bertie," went on Valeria. "I don't know if the Greendalers would kill you or not. Probably not. But there are ways to make you do anything Bess Udall wants."

"Would she dare?" inquired Davis.

"Since you failed to do anything yesterday but run away . . . yes. Claudia was talking about red-hot pincers. I heard her."

Davis didn't think she was lying.

He glanced up at Minos. The big planet was almost half full. It wasn't as bright by day, but he could see clearly . . . the amber face blurred by a crushingly thick atmosphere, hydrogen with the vapors of water, methane, ammonia; cloudy bands across the face, dull green, blue, brown; dark blots which were storms big enough to swallow Earth whole; the shadow of an outer moon. He shivered. It was a long and lonesome way home. Light would need two centuries to reach the nearest civilization; the Service didn't plan to visit Delta for another generation.

He didn't think he could survive that long. He *had* to get his boat back, through the Doctors or through the Whitley scheme of finding allies. He knew that Bess Udall of Greendale—or her opposite number in the allied towns, whichever of them beat out the rest in the inevitable war—wouldn't give him a chance to escape.

In short, I have no choice. I'm on the Whitley team.

He looked at the cousins and then at Elinor; she smiled back at him. It could be a lot worse, he thought complacently.

60

CHAPTER IX

During the first two weeks—or one week, if you counted by Earth days—they traveled hard. Once they heard horns blowing, and hid in a cave for a day; Elinor whimpered her terrified way into Davis' arms, but he was too worried to enjoy it.

Otherwise it was steady riding, by sunlight and Minoslight, with three or four hours of rest in the twelve. Davis was in fairly good condition, but keeping the saddle aboard an orsper required muscles he had never heard of, and said muscles objected strenuously. Elinor was too numb even to complain much.

They lived off the country. It was not the season for nuts or berries; game was plentiful, but Davis wearied of the carnivorous diet. Ordinarily he and Elinor would keep the trail with one Whitley, while the other went off to bag the day's rations. A feeling of uselessness oppressed him.

He did try out the arbalest that was part of the equipment at his saddlebow. It was a cleverly engineered piece of work; the original design must be due to some early castaway who had given up trying to find the ingredients of gunpowder. (Presumably the Ship had carried no firearms; a colony shuttle wouldn't normally.) A chamber holding six short iron-tipped quarrels fed them automatically into the slot; a tightly wound spring furnished energy enough to recock the bow several times. It was a hard-hitting, accurate weapon with a high rate of fire, and Davis knew enough gunnery to become good with it.

But Valeria told him coldly that he made entirely too much noise to help stalk game.

Freetoon lay in mere foothills compared to the range which now lifted before them. It rose steep and terrific, with a long barren stretch above timberline, deep in snow

61

and scoured by glaciers. There were no paths, and the Whitleys had to guess at a route toward the pass, of which they knew only by hearsay.

Slowly his frame adapted, and he began to feel some surplus energy. On the last night below timberline he offered to stand a watch. They intended to rest through the whole darkness, gathering strength for the push over the range.

"Well . . ." Valeria looked doubtful. "No, we don't need that. Anything could sneak up on you."

Barbara frowned. "That's not fair, Val," she said. "Davis may not be used to this land, but he's stronger than we are. I could use a little extra sleep."

"Oh, very well." Her cousin laughed. "No jacklins or wolfers around, so let him have his fun."

Davis felt grateful to Barbara. He wasn't sure whether she really meant what she said. Maybe it had been only to spite Valeria; maybe she felt his ego needed a shot. But it did, that was the fact, and she had spoken gently.

The women rolled up in their blankets and went to sleep. Davis pulled on the crude jerkin Barbara had stitched together for him, drew his cloak over that, and stretched numb feet toward the fire. His sandals were falling apart, and there were no boots for him.

It was a cloudy night. Davis had a glimpse of Theseus, nearly fully above Minos, a ruddy moon hazed by its own thin atmosphere, seeming to fly between great wind-driven darknesses. His telescope had spotted signs of intelligent life there, too, he thought wistfully, but of course he had landed on Atlantis before visiting an ocherous Mars-like pill.

He poked up the small fire for what little comfort it could give. A few dry snowflakes gusted across his vision. The scrubby growth crowded around him, demonic with thorns, branches twisted and creaking. Something far away made an idiot laughter noise.

The dim ember-glow picked out Barbara's face . . . or was it Valeria's? No, the left hand was out of the blankets and lacked a healing scar. Barbara, then. She looked curiously innocent as she slept. Elinor looked voluptuous even through the bedroll, but Elinor snored.

No coffee and no tobacco closer than his ship, and it

62

was ringed with spears. Davis commiserated his own poor lonely harried self. He began to nod, jerked back awake, swore, and indulged thoughts of champagne, baby shrimp mayonnaise, mutant oysters, boeuf tartare—oops! He discovered that he had lost all taste for boeuf tartare.

"Peep," said a voice.

"Yipe!" said Davis. He grabbed for his bow.

The peeper stepped daintily into view. It was a fluffy little bird, round as a butterball, with a parrot bill and large pathetic eyes. Davis thought of potting it—no, they had meat enough already and the bird was settling happily down beside him. It liked the fire, he guessed. He ventured to pat it, and the peeper wriggled with pleasure.

"Sure, make yourself at home," whispered Davis. "There's a nice bird. I need someone to talk to. I feel lonesome."

"Peep," said the peeper sympathetically.

Davis chatted to it till he began to grow uncontrollaby sleepy. Better let Valeria take over. He reached his toes across the firecoals and nudged her with a certain malicious pleasure.

"Oh . . . oh, yes." The girl yawned and rolled out of her blanket. "Nothing much—*Hoy!*" She froze where she stood.

"Oh, this?" Davis stroked the peeper, which had cuddled on his lap. "Meet George W. Came in, and . . ."

Valeria was quite pale. "Don't move," she breathed through stiffened lips. "Don't move for your life."

Her hand stole to her belt; very very slowly, she withdrew a dart. "When I kill it, roll away. Understand? *Now!*"

The missile leaped from her hand and skewered the peeper. Davis scrambled to get free of its death throes. "What the . . ." he shouted.

Barbara and Elinor sat up. Elinor screamed.

Valeria let out a rattling laugh. "That thing has a bite with enough poison to kill ten people."

Davis made no reply.

"You're relieved from further watch duty," snapped Valeria. "Get to sleep now—if you can!"

"That's all right," said Barbara as he slunk to his bedroll. "You couldn't know, could you?"

63

"And the more fools us, for not realizing it," snorted Valeria. "Him a Man? Hah!"

In the morning they saddled up and started over the pass. The tongue of a glacier had to be crossed, and the orspers registered a protest which landed Davis and Elinor in the snow. The Whitleys beat the birds into submission, deftly avoiding kicks which might have disembowelled them.

Davis couldn't really blame the orspers. They had such large bare feet. After a few hours, it seemed like forever since he had been warm.

They were still under the pass when they made a miserable camp, huddled together for warmth. The next day was spent crossing, hard-packed snow underfoot and bleak blue-gray walls on either side and wind hooting in their faces. The acrid smoke of a nearby volcano stung their eyes. Barbara worried aloud about the condition of the mounts. "Jaded, chilblained, limping, half-starved. We'll have to give them a rest when we're down in the woods again."

The range dropped even more steeply on the north side. From the pass, Davis looked across a downward-rolling immensity of green, veined by rivers, here and there the flash of a lake. He wished for his paints, to capture the scene. He could make out no signs of cultivation, but there must be some; his telescopic cameras had registered small clearings and dots which might be houses.

"Haven't you any idea what the people down there are like?" he asked. "Seems like you'd all meet at the Ship."

"No," said Elinor. "You see, Bertie, each town sends its own parties to be fertilized, by their own route. It's seldom that two groups are at the Ship at the same time, and even if they are, they don't talk to anyone but— Oh, I mustn't say more."

"Hm. What about an escort? Couldn't such a party be attacked?"

"Oh, no. Everybody knows that a procession bound for the Ship, with their flags and their tribute and gifts and everything . . . well, we're holy. Going or coming on such an errand, we mustn't be hurt. If somebody did attack us, why, the Doctors would refuse to fertilize that whole town forever after."

64

Which would be one form of excommunication that really worked, thought Davis. He gave Elinor a sidelong glance. Her nose was frostbitten and peeling. She had lost weight, but she was still an interesting lesson in solid geometry. And he wanted a lot more information from her, whether it was taboo to non-initiates or not. He was going to enjoy persuading her.

Meanwhile, though, they had to get down where it was warm.

Later he remembered the next two days only as a nightmare of struggle. He could hardly believe it when they reached timberline and the nearly vertical descent began to flatten.

This was a conifer forest, widely spaced trees looking not unlike jack pines, though the smell was different, sweeter and headier. The ground was thick with brown needles, tall trunks and lichenous boulders thrusting out of it, the orsper footfalls a muted *pad-pad*. They saw only small, noisy birds, darting red and gold between bluish-green branches, but there was spoor of big game.

Even Davis could see how worn the orspers were. There was no choice; they had to rest.

At the end of the day, they reached a king-sized lake. It blinked amiably in the low sunshine, reeds rustled on the banks and fish leaped in the water. "We couldn't find a better campsite, I think," said Barbara.

"Skeeterbugs," said Valeria.

"Not this early in the year."

"Yeh? Look here, rockhead, I've seen skeeterbugs when . . ."

While the cousins argued, Davis dismounted. Elinor looked down at him. "Oh, I'm so tired," she said.

"*Allons!* Leap, my pretty one." Davis held out his arms. She giggled and jumped into them.

Either she was more hefty or he was weaker than he'd thought. They went over together, rolling down the slope. The position in which they ended was rather compromising.

Elinor wriggled. "I'm all dizzee-ee," she said. "Let me up."

"Not just yet," grinned Davis.

"Oh . . . Bertie, stop! Oh! Oh, you're so . . ."

Valeria stormed into view. She tossed her axe. It thunked in the ground among Elinor's tresses. "We camp here," she yelled. "Get up, you lazy frump, and give us a hand!"

Davis reached a final decision. He did not like Valeria. There were no skeeterbugs. This did not improve Valeria's temper.

The orspers needed plenty of food to recover their health. In the morning, both Whitleys went out afoot after game, planning to be gone most of the day. Davis and Elinor were to watch the camp and try for fish: there were hooks and lines in the saddlebags, floats and poles were easily cut though Valeria fumed at putting her axe to such menial use.

Davis watched the twins leave, Barbara headed east and Valeria west. It was a cool, sun-drenched day and a flock of birds with particularly good voices were tuning up nearby. Davis' grin spread.

"What are you so happy about?" Elinor looked rather grimly up from the utensils she had been scouring.

"At having you all to myself." He knew her type.

"Oh, now . . . Bertie! There may be the most awful things around . . ."

"For you I would gladly face dragons," said Davis, "though of course I'd rather face you. Let's take a stroll." He jerked his thumb at the tethered orspers. "I never saw anything stare the way those overgrown chickens do."

"Bertie!" Elinor pouted. "I'm so tired. I just want to sleep."

"As you wish." He sauntered off. In a moment she pattered after him. He took her hand, squeezing it rather more than necessary.

"Bertie! Bertie, be careful, you're so *strong* . . ."

Davis wandered eastward along the lakeshore, eyes alert for a secluded spot. He was in no hurry; all day before him, and he was going to enjoy the fishing, too. Hadn't fished for years.

"You're a brave little girl, Elinor," he said. "Coming all this way and . . ." he paused, took a deep breath, and prepared the Big Lie . . . . "never a complaint from you."

"I could complain," she said bitterly. "Those awful

66

Whitleys. Skin and bones and nasty red hair and tongues like files. They're just jealous."

It would have been profitable to agree, but for some reason Davis couldn't backbite Barbara. "It's a long way to go yet," he said, "but I hope the worst is over. You ought to tell me what to expect when we reach the Ship."

"I can't, Bertie. I mustn't. Nobody who's been there is allowed to talk about it to anyone who hasn't. It's too holy for children."

"But I'm not a child," he argued. "I am, in fact, a Man. You do believe that, don't you?"

"Yes . . . you must be . . . even if your whiskers *tickle*."

Davis stroked his short yellow beard patriarchally. It had become gratifyingly thick. "Well, then," he said, "the Doctors are only, uh, filling in for Men . . . I mean . . . Sunblaze!" He backed up and started over. "What are they like, the Doctors?"

"I can't . . ." Davis stopped for some agreeable physical persuasion . . . "I mustn't—mmmmm—Bertie!" After a while: "I really *can't* say. They have this big beautiful town, with the Ship in the very middle. There's a causeway over the swamps. But I never saw a Doctor. They're always veiled."

Davis was struck by a ghastly suspicion. "But they *are* women, aren't they?" he barked.

"Oh, yes. Yes, I could see that much. Bertie, please! I *mustn't* tell you anything."

"I can guess. The, uh, fertilizing rite—it involves a machine, doesn't it? A lot of tubes and wires and things?"

"If you know that much," said Elinor, "yes." She made a wry face. "I didn't like that part. It hurt a little, and it was so scary. But the other rites are beautiful."

Davis nodded absently. The picture was taking shape.

Three hundred years ago, the hyperdrive was new and colonization more art than science. You couldn't trust an apparently Earthlike planet; chances were its biochemistry would be lethal to man. It was rare good luck to find a world like Atlantis.

Even apparently habitable planets might harbor some unsuspected germ to which man had no immunity. First a planet was thoroughly surveyed. Then an all-male party landed, spent two or three years building, analyzing, testing. Finally the women came.

He didn't know the history of Atlantis' Ship. Somewhere in the Service archives lay a record of a female transport with a female crew—you didn't mix the sexes on such a journey unless you wanted trouble. Judging from the names and the fragments of Christian belief, its complement had been purely North American; regional distinctions had still been considered important in those days. The Ship was bound for a new colony, but it vanished. A trepidation vortex, of course—perhaps the same one he had so narrowly missed. That was back before anyone knew of such a thing.

The Ship had not been destroyed. It had been tossed at an unthinkable pseudovelocity across two hundred or more light-years. The hyperdrive must have been ruined, since it didn't return home. But it must have emerged quite near Delta Capitis Lupi.

Pure good fortune that Atlantis was habitable. Doubtless the humans landed without preliminary tests they were not equipped to make . . . nothing to lose. Probably the Ship had been wrecked; they were cut off, no way to call for help and no way to get back.

They had little machinery, no weapons, scant technical knowledge. The crew must have done what they could, but you can't reproduce blasters and nuclear converters without certain machines. They discovered what the edible grains and the domesticable fowl were, set up a primitive agriculture, located iron and copper mines and established crude smelters, named the planet and moons in classical tradition . . . but that was all, and their knowledge slipped from them in a few illiterate lifetimes.

But in the first generation there had been a biochemist. There must have been. The thought of growing old and dying, one by one, with nobody to help the last feeble survivors, was unwelcome. Human parthenogenesis was an ancient technique. The biochemist had taken what equipment was in the Ship to make such a machine.

The right chemicals under the right conditions would cause a single ovum to divide. Once that process was initiated, it followed the normal course, and in nine months a child was born, genetically identical with the mother.

68

"It's an appalling situation," said Davis. "It will have to be remedied."

"What are you talking about?"

"You'll find out," he grinned.

They had come to a little bay, with soft grass down to the water's edge, rustling shade trees, the mountains looming titanic above. Flowers blossomed fiery underfoot and small waves chuckled against the shore. There must be a sheer drop-off here to unknown depths, the water was so dark. But its surface glinted silver.

It was, in short, an ideal spot for romance.

Davis planted his fishing pole in a forked twig, the hook baited with a strip of jerky. He laid aside his bow and the axe Barbara had lent him, sat down, and extended an invitational arm.

Elinor sighed and snuggled up to him.

"Just think," she whispered. "The first Man in three hundred years!"

"High time, isn't it?" Davis gathered her in. She closed her eyes, breathing hard.

Davis laid a hand on her knee. She didn't object, so he slipped it upward. Elinor moaned a little. Her own hands moved along his back and hips, and around again. "Oh!" she exclaimed. "Your kilt—what's happening?"

"If you want a demonstration—" he leered.

"I do, I do." She wriggled. "I'm so *interested!*"

He let her glide downward in his embrace, until she lay on the grass. She clasped his neck, pulling his head toward hers. "Hold me close," she whispered.

"Just a minute and I will." He fumbled with her belt buckle.

Something roared behind him.

Davis leaped a meter in the air. Elinor shrieked.

The thing looked like a saw-beaked, penguin-feathered seal, but bigger. It had swallowed his hook and was quite indignant. The flippers shot it up on the shore and over the grass at express speed.

Elinor tried to get to her feet. The fluke-like legs batted out. She went rolling and lay still. Davis clawed for his axe. The beak closed on his left ankle. He chopped wildly, saw blood run, but the soft iron wouldn't bite on that thick skull . . .

The seal-bird knocked him down, held him with one flipper and snapped at his face. Jaws closed on the axe haft and crunched it across. Davis got a hand on the upper and lower mandibles. Somehow he struggled free, threw a leg over the long sleek back and heaved. The brute roared and writhed. He felt his strength pour out of him, the teeth were closing on his fingers.

A crossbow bolt hummed and buried itself in the wet flank. Another and another—Barbara ran over the grass, shooting as she went. The monster turned its head and Davis yanked his hands free.

"Get away!" yelled Barbara.

Her bow was empty now. She crouched, drawing her knife, and plunged toward the creature. It reared up, roaring. She jammed her left arm under its beak, forced the head back, and slashed.

The flippers churned, and the seal-bird bowled her over. Davis glimpsed a slim leg beneath the belly. He picked up his own bow and fired pointblank, hardly aware of what he did. Blood gurgled in the monster's voice.

Then it slumped, and the arterial spurting was only a red flow across slippery grass.

"Barbara . . ." Davis tugged at the weight, feeble and futile. His own throat rattled.

The leg stirred. Barbara forced her way out from under.

She stood up, gasping, and stared at him. Blood ran from her face and breast and arms, dripped to the ground, she stood in a puddle of blood. Davis' knees gave way.

"Are you all right?" she whispered. "Bert, darling, are you all right?" She stumbled toward him.

"Yeh . . ." He had a nasty gash in the ankle, and his palms were lacerated, but it was nothing serious. "You?"

"Oh, th-th-this isn't my blood." She laughed shortly, sank to her knees before him, and burst into tears.

"There, there." He patted the bronze head, clumsy and unsure of himself. "It's all over, Barbara, it's finished now . . . Sunblaze, we've got meat for the pot . . ."

She shook herself, wiped her eyes, and gave him an angry stare. "You *fool!*" she snuffled. "If I hadn't h-h-happened to be near . . . heard the noise . . . oh, you blind gruntbrain!"

"Guess I've got that coming;" said Davis. "Why do you drag me along, anyway?"

"I don't know," said Barbara, rising. "Get up!"

Elinor stirred, looked around, and started to cry. Since she wasn't much hurt, she got no attention. "Well!" she muttered.

Barbara swallowed her rage. "I never saw a thing like this before," she admitted. "I suppose you couldn't have known, Bert. You were giving it a good fight."

"Thanks," he said uncomfortably.

"And as you said . . . plenty of meat." She squared her shoulders. "I'll stand guard. You take Elinor back to camp, and when Valeria returns we can all drag it back."

"Yes," said Davis weakly. "I guess that's best."

CHAPTER X

When Valeria had blown off enough pressure by a magnificent description of Davis' intelligence, education, and personality, she offered news. There were clear signs of nearby settlement to the west: recent campsites, a beaten trail, smoke rising over the treetops. "They'll be sure to find us," she said, "and it mightn't look so well that we didn't go directly to them."

"Oh, yes!" babbled Elinor. "We can't stay here, those *things* in the lake . . ." Valeria glared her into silence.

Barbara's eyes gleamed. "And maybe we can make a deal with them. By the time we get home with help, the allies will have fallen apart, and our own messmates in the woods will join us. Let's go!"

"In the morning, child," said Valeria.

"Don't call me a child!" shouted Barbara. "I'm only three days younger than you, and my brain is twenty years older!"

"Girls, girls," began Davis. Then he apparently thought better of it and sat back to listen.

His injuries throbbed abominably, but sheer exhaustion put him to sleep. At Bee-rise he was able to limp around and help Barbara re-haft her axe.

She regarded him with concern. He had seemed such a big coward, she reflected . . . and yet he didn't try to run from the lake bird, but saved Elinor's life— Damn Elinor, anyway! If Davis had died on her account— And he had crossed an unimaginable chill gulf of distance, to a world hidden from all his people. Maybe it was only that he had never been trained as she had been. The concept of cultural difference was a new one; she knotted her brows over it. How would a Man, surrounded by robots, fire-shooting weapons, orsperless wagons, buildings as high as mountains, how would he think?

But it was heresy to admit this creature, barely two meters tall, who could sweat and bleed and be afraid, was a Man!

Then the Men were a thing colder and more remote than she had realized. Davis was *here*, warm and breathing. She could smell the faint pungency of his skin; his beard was like spun gold in the early sunlight and his eyes were blue with the most fascinating crinkles when he laughed. Yes, he sang her a bouncy little song as they worked, and laughed with her, which was beneath the dignity of the stony Men.

His hand brushed her knee, accidentally, and for a moment it seemed to burn and the world wobbled. What was wrong with her? She wanted to laugh and cry at the same time. She had cried yesterday, something no Whitley did past the age of twelve.

"Damn!" said Barbara.

"What's the matter?" asked Davis.

"Oh, nothing. Leave me alone, will you?" Then: "No, I didn't mean that!"

Davis gave her a very long look. She couldn't meet it, she wanted to squirm. Savagely, she finished whittling the handle and put it through the axhead. Davis held it while she drove in the wedge with a stone, concentrating furiously on the work.

Valeria, somewhat handicapped by Elinor's assistance, had butchered the lake bird. Its hide might be a valuable gift to the Udall where they were bound. She loaded the orspers evenly and said the party had better walk to spare them.

"Except Davis," said Barbara.

"Never mind Davis!" said Valeria.

Barbara swung her axe so it whistled. The new shaft was carved from a seasoned branch and felt strong enough. "We started out to snatch him away from the enemy," she answered stiffly. "Now he's got a hurt leg. What's the point of having him along at all, you clothead, if we don't take care of him?"

"Have it your way," shrugged her cousin.

They went slowly along the shore. Davis swapped mounts from time to time. Toward evening they found a hard-packed path through a meadow, and could see a curl of smoke against sinking Theseus.

Barbara glanced uneasily into the shadowed forest and hefted her crossbow. She had a sense of being watched

. . . yes, the songbirds were too quiet. Well . . . "This road seems headed for the town," she said. "We can follow it."

Whoever paced them between the trees was a skilled tracker. Barbara grew certain there was somebody.

And this silent following was not the way of the folk who dwelt near Holy River. Barbara shuddered, remembering dark stories mumbled by the helots, Critters and Gobblies. She found herself edging closer to Davis.

They rounded a bend, where a growth of canebrake hid what lay beyond, and met the strangers.

There were half a dozen, mounted, their shadows long and black ahead of them. They were all Burkes: tall slender women with dark, close-cropped hair and blue eyes; the faces were a bit too long, but the wide brows and pert noses would have been pretty if the lips were not so thin. At home Burkes were soldiers, artists and artisans in peacetime—not very popular, because of their habit of coming up with unconventional ideas, but often made Udall counselors.

These bore arbalests, javelins, and a weapon at the belt new to Barbara, a curved knife a meter long, obviously meant for slashing from orsperback. They were peculiarly dressed, in cloth trousers, puff-sleeved shirts, leather doublets with some distinguishing mark branded on each.

There was a noise behind Barbara. She whirled and saw another dozen coming from the woods, ringing in her party. More Burkes!

Valeria lifted empty hands. "We're from Freetoon over the mountains," she said. "We come in peace."

The oldest woman, about fifty but still lithe, rode a way ahead of her troop. "Over Smoky Pass?" She spoke with a clipped accent, hard to follow. "Why? What's this with you?"

Davis nodded genially. "I am a Man," he said.

"Hm?" The Burkes looked hard at him. They did not break into chatter among themselves, as Freetooners would have done.

"Man?" snapped the oldest one. "Where from?"

Davis pointed to the sky. "Up there, the stars." He beamed at them. "I'm the genuine article. Beware of imitations."

There was a long silence. It was disconcerting.

74

"What d'you want?" asked somebody.

"We'll discuss that with your Udall," said Valeria haughtily.

"Our . . . oh. No Udall. Talk to Council. Come."

No Udall! Barbara was too stunned to do more than follow meekly as the riders urged her forward.

"But this is awful," whispered Elinor. She trembled.

Davis narrowed his eyes. "Wait a minute," he said. "Is there anyone but your sort around here?"

The leader smiled. "No. Burkes of Burkeville. I'm Gwen, army chief."

"Not much of an army," said Valeria brashly.

She received a scornful look. "Don't need much. War's stupid. If we're attacked, ev'ry Burke fights."

Nothing more was said. Barbara felt bewildered. *Of course,* she thought numbly, *of course if they are all Burkes they can all bear arms. But no Udall? How do they decide what to do?* Then, after wrestling with the matter: *I suppose they must all want much the same thing, so it can't be a great problem for them.*

Both suns were down and Minos well into the second quarter when they reached Burkeville. There was light enough to see by. The town was built on piles in a narrow bay of the lake, some fifty long buildings of planed lumber and shingled roofs, in a graceful, airy, riotously carved and painted style. Slim boats were moored to the piles, with masts and furled sails—not that Barbara recognized that item. There was a drawbridge for crossing ten meters of open water, it thudded beneath the orsper feet.

Word must have gone ahead. Burkes of all ages stood in front of their barracks. They spoke little to each other, which seemed unnatural to Barbara. Here and there, above the plank deck of the town, rose tall wooden statues. They seemed to be stylized representations of humans and animals in violent action. A smell of fish told her that Burkeville got most of its food from the lake, probably had only a few small fields on shore . . . yes, they could barter . . .

About two thousand adults, she estimated through the blue night, and as many children. All were scantily clad and had their hair cut short.

The party stopped before a house in the middle of

town. They entered without formality, leaving the doors open so the rest of the women could look in. A line of red pillars carved with vines and birds marched down the hall. There was a fireplace, but most of the light came from bracketed candles—the room was positively brilliant. And beautiful, thought Barbara, looking at the chairs and tables, the feather tapestries and copper plaques.

Indoors there was an even more casual attitude toward clothes than at Freetoon. Most of the women wore little more than a few beads. Davis' eyes shuttled. Barbara felt a thick anger. She could show these snake-hipped, flat-chested creatures a thing or two!

Several mature women sprawled in the big chairs near the hearth. They rose and stared at Davis. He grew uncomfortable after a minute. "Hello," he said.

"Greetings." The one who spoke was a trifle more ornamented than the rest, with a feather skirt and a plume in her hair. She was in her thirties. "Kathleen the Second. I speak for Council. Sit."

Davis lowered himself, shaking a dazed head. "What goes on here? I don't understand. Are you nothing but, uh, Burkes?"

"Right. Live as we want to. Ever'body else stupid." Kathleen gave the Whitleys a challenging glance; both of them flushed but decided not to make an issue of it. "Began hun'erd years 'go, Flormead overrun an' sev'ral Burkes got away t'gether."

"I see. Well . . ."

" 'Bout y'selves. Oh, y'll wan' food, drink." Kathleen nodded to a few adolescents who stood nearby. They went out, silently. "Glad see you. Only rumors 'bout other side of the mountains."

Valeria cleared her throat. "We come as refugees, ma'am," she said with the proper blend of pride and deference. " But not as beggars. Our arms are at our hostess' service, and if you will accept a small gift, the hide of a great bird we killed yesterday . . ."

The hall rang with laughter. Valeria jumped to her feet.

" 'Scuse." Kathleen wiped her eyes. "Not our custom. Story goes y' have chiefs an' such silliness. Correct? Like certain folk on this side, s'pose."

"What else would we have?" asked Barbara, bridling.

76

"We all think same way. Natural. Council makes routine decisions. It don' make Councilors any better'n anyone else. Ah!"

The girls were returning with laden trays. Davis, Barbara, and Valeria attacked the food hungrily. Elinor minded her manners. The drink was merely unfermented berry juice; Barbara recalled that *her* Burkes didn't like beer. Kathleen and the others watched them.

"Now, then," said the Speaker when they had finished. "Who're you?" She looked at Davis.

"Davis Bertram," he smiled. "A Man . . . a human male."

There was a rushing of whispers, but only from the children.

So he says! thought Barbara. She was about to blurt how he lied, but shut her lips. Valeria's snapped closed at the same time. It would be helpful if the Burkes were convinced.

"Story?" said Kathleen at last. Her face was impassive. Davis sketched it for her.

There was another stillness. Heads shook, slowly, and the slim bodies shifted. A few spears were raised beyond the door.

"Wait," said Kathleen. "This is new . . . have t' think . . . Can y' prove it?"

"Of course," said Davis smugly. Barbara wanted to slap him.

"Hmmm . . . we never thought highly o' stories, handed out from Ship. If Men're human males, means they're human—like us—no more." Kathleen traded looks with her twins. " 'Stonishing. Hard t' swallow, but—" Abruptly: "What y' plans?"

"We were seeking to help to win back Freetoon," said Barbara.

There was another rain of laughter.

"Not int'rested," said Kathleen. "What's a mixed town t' us?"

"We're going to the Ship,' added Davis.

"Hm . . . yes. I see." Kathleen rose. "Y're tired now. Welcome here. Talk t'morrow."

It was a dismissal.

77

CHAPTER XI

The Burkes lived in barracks like the Freetooners, but there was no caste distinction. Barbara was led to a house as ornamented as the Council room. The decorations lacked a master plan; each woman had her own stretch of wall above a low bed and did what she wished to it, but the overall effect was of harmonious repetition. There were a few vacant bunks, luxurious after the straw ticks of Freetoon and the bedrolls of the march.

The morning bustle woke her. She joined the rest in a chow line, where cooks were dishing up bread and fried fish. It could almost have been home, save that the KP's were also Burkes.

"How do they settle who does the cooking?" she wondered aloud.

"All take turns at menial work," said a townswoman. "Otherwise carry on our sep'rate trades."

The fishing fleet had already set forth. Elsewhere Burkes carved, painted, wove, and there was one who sat with a harp composing a song. Barbara shook her head. "They can't do all that!"

"Any gifted person can do a lot of things," Davis told her. "I know two brothers, identical twins, on Earth. One is a psycho-technician and one a spaceship captain. And both of them play second fiddle in an amateur orchestra. I myself am a painter of sorts."

"Oh, an *artist!*" squealed Elinor.

Davis seemed less interested in her today. At least he had taste enough to go for the Burkes, thought Barbara resentfully . . . not that that was saying much. There were some children swimming gaily between the piles; the lake monsters must have learned this bay was unsafe for them. Davis looked at cool, glistening water, stripped, and

78

plunged. After a moment, the Whitleys followed suit.

Davis was a good swimmer. He shouted, dove under, and got a grip on Barbara's ankle. She came up again sputtering. He appeared beside her, grinned, and planted a kiss on her lips.

"Don't!" she gasped.

"Why not? Confidentially, you and Val are the best-built wenches on Atlantis."

"Stop that!" said Valeria. "We're on trial here. I don't like this situation one tiny bit."

She swam off with long smooth strokes. Davis eyed her sullenly. Barbara used the chance to escape . . . *escape from what?* she wondered. There was still a cold damp tingle on her mouth.

Afterward they sat on the deck, drying, while Burkes clustered around. There were eager questions, and their own queries were answered freely enough. But Barbara noticed a sort of relay, her words being passed through the crowd toward the Council hall. It gave her an uneasy feeling.

The Burkes talked little among themselves, she noticed; no reason for conversation, ordinarily. There was something pyschic about this place, she decided—she had never feared any woman, not even the Old Udall, but these Burkes were too alien for comfort.

"An' y're really a Man?" asked a young girl. The children here were a brash lot, above a curious inward restraint.

Davis nodded. "I am. But as Kathleen put it, I'm only human."

Valeria and Barbara looked at each other. Chattering like a baby! The blind chickwit! If he would only act as a Man should, they would have had a chance to overawe all Burkeville.

An older woman frowned. "We ne'er gave much heed t' old tales," she said. "Burkes think f'r 'emselves. Must'a been shipwreck, f' natural reasons, in old days . . ."

"That's right," said Davis.

"Doctors have power because only Doctors can fertilize. We tried t' build fertilizing machine. No luck. So we have t' pay tribute an' go through their silly rites like ever'body else."

"Oh!" whispered Elinor. "Talking about it in front of . . . of *children!*"

"So y've initiations on y'r side mountains? Big secret. Jus' like swampfolk. We all grow up knowing truth."

Barbara's universe, already somewhat battered, quivered and lost a few more bricks. These Burkes broke every law in the canon and throve. Could it be that Father was not behind the Doctors?

She waited for a thunderbolt. None came. Defiantly, she repeated the thought. Glancing over her own tanned form, she saw no shriveling.

But then, she thought wildly, then everything Davis claimed made sense! Then he might actually *be* a Man!

Vaguely, through a clamorous heartbeat, she heard the dry Burke voice: " 'Course, we don' tell Doctors what we think. Raise our kids t' keep mouth shut when legates arrive."

"Sensible girls," said Davis.

He was dry now, and resumed his kilt and cloak. The Whitleys wound up their wet hair and did likewise. They were all guided around town, shown the sights; the peace and plenty of Burkeville were bragged up for them, and Barbara had to admit there was truth in the boasts.

"But the life must be dull," she murmured to Valeria. The cousins had found an excuse to wander off by themselves; interest was all centered on Davis. "The same person, over and over."

"A pretty many-sided person, though."

"Yes . . . Val, I was just thinking . . . we, our way of living, it may have shrunk us somehow. Everybody knowing just one thing, one skill—any of these Burkes can talk about anything."

"You may be right," nodded Valeria. "I've had much the same notions today, and Father didn't kill me for having them. But I don't think the Burkes are any better than us, not really."

"Mmmm . . . yes. I see what you mean. They make all these pretty carvings and things, but one piece of art is so much like another. And they miss all the fun of talking to somebody different. Remember how we used to argue with Kim and Ginny?"

Sudden tears stung her eyes. Sharp before her rose

80

Freetoon—but it was done, finished, dead. Even if she returned in triumph, drove out the enemy and found all her friends still alive for her it could not be the same, it was too narrow and lonesome.

She could never go home.

She wanted to find Davis and blurt her woe to him.

"It would be better if the Men came," said Valeria softly. "We've never lived as Father—or whoever made the stars—meant us to live. We've just hung on, hoping, for three hundred years."

Barbara felt a smile tug at her mouth. "It would be fun to have a Man-child," she mused. Then, in stabbing realization: "But Val! Bert *is* a Man!"

"Rotten specimen of one," snapped Valeria.

Barbara felt puzzled. They thought so much alike that it was hard to see why Val despised Davis.

Her mind wandered back to the Man, and she forgot the question.

"Better get back," said Valeria. "I don't trust that Davis out of my sight."

Elinor was seated outside their barrack. She looked small and scared. No one else was around; the Burkes had again clustered by the Council hall.

"Where's Davis?" asked Barbara. Her throat felt tight.

"In there." Elinor pointed to the house. "They sent for him . . . that Kathleen!" She looked up, her eyes wide. "When are we getting out of this awful place?"

"As soon as possible," said Valeria grimly. "Whenever that may be. No help here, and I wouldn't put anything past them."

Elinor began to cry, noisily wishing herself back with darling Claudia. The Whitleys glared at her and moved away.

"I'd give a lot to hear what's being said," whispered Valeria. "If we weren't asked to join . . . it doesn't look so good for us."

"Maybe they didn't think of it." Barbara ran across booming planks to the edge of the crowd. "Let me in, please."

"Sorry, no." An armed Burke waved a saber. "Private discussion."

"What's private *here*?" flared Barbara.

81

Other trousered warriors moved closer. The sunlight was hot on their spearheads. Barbara cursed and returned to the barrack.

"I think we could make a break for it," said Valeria. "That bridge is still down, and there are fresh orspers just across the street. Nobody's looking."

"What good would that do?" countered Barbara. "Without Davis, we're nothing but outlaws. But if I could listen . . ."

The close-packed Burkes were whispering, relaying to each other what was said within the hall. The younger ones kept glancing furtively at the Freetooners.

"Come inside," said Barbara. "I have an idea."

The emptiness of the barrack was welcome after all those eyes. There was a trapdoor on the floor, opening on the lake; the Burkes sometimes liked to fish through it, or you could throw stones down on enemy boats. "I think I can get at the hall this way," said Barbara. "Nobody's on the other side of it."

"I'll go," said Valeria.

"You will *not!* I thought of it first!"

"Yeh . . . and somebody has to watch this." Valeria gave Elinor an unfriendly stare. "Go, then. If they set on me, I've got my axe, and I can stand them off for a while."

Barbara removed her clothes and opened the trap. She hung by her fingers . . . the water was three meters below. Valeria grinned tightly and handed her a lasso from her kit. Barbara went down it cautiously and began to swim.

Sunlight and shadow streamed between the piles. Through clear water, she could see a weedy bottom and fish sliding over stones. The sails of the fleet shone red and blue across five kilometers, the forest was green beyond and the sky brilliant overhead. It was very near eclipse.

She waited until Bee went behind Minos. Ay still threw a feeble light, the planet glowed ghostly and banded, but a dense dusk flowed across the world. Barbara swarmed up the ladder at the far end of the deck. She could barely see the crowd on the opposite side of the hall. Their light cloaks glimmered. Her own sun-darkened form must be invisible at this distance.

82

Business did not halt for eclipse . . . had those witches no respect for anything? Barbara ran across the planks, dodging from house to house. The hall was before her. She glided to one of its large windows and peered carefully in.

There were only a few Burkes speaking directly to Davis. All but Kathleen were old: their most experienced Councilors. Candles had been lit against the eclipse, and Davis towered splendidly in the glow.

He spoke, and Barbara thought—even now—what a fine thing a deep voice was. Whitleys were contraltos, but these Burkes were all yattering sopranos, and . . .

"All right, Kate, so I've convinced you I am a Man."

"Not entirely. Still need final proof." She didn't even blush!

"Sure! Whenever we can get some privacy."

"Oh, y' wish t' be alone? Very well."

"Who will . . . er . . ."

"I—If all goes well, if I'm not hurt—"

"You won't be." Davis was grinning like a foolfish.

"Good."

Kathleen slipped off her mantle and let it fall at her feet. She wasn't wearing anything beneath. She stood up straight, throwing her shoulders back and bosom forward. *Well, she's got to make the most of what she has!* thought Barbara. But then, driven by a stubborn realism: *What she has isn't so bad. Not really. She's too thin, but nothing haggard about her. She has the muscles to bounce around as readily as anyone.*

She thought: *Davis sees that also,* and wondered why tears blurred her vision.

Kathleen caught the Man's hands between her own and looked up at him. "B'lieve kissing cust'mary 'mong mixed-fam'ly tribes," she said.

Davis glanced at the impassive audience, shrugged a little, grinned one-sided, and pulled Kathleen against him. She placed his palms on her flanks and hugged his neck. As their lips met, Barbara told herself with an oath that she would *not* bawl.

"Pleas'rable," said Kathleen. "See potential'ties of an elab'rated technique in this. What methods d'y' rec'mmend?"

"Well, uh, you might try moving around a little," choked Davis.

She writhed. Her fingers stroked him experimentally, sensitive to his own response. As he came up for air, Davis gasped: "Great Cosmos! I n-n-never expected—an intellectual like you—would—"

"All arts best when an'lyzed." Kathleen was as flushed as he, starting to breathe hard. "Once I get a background o' 'sperience, I might . . . yes . . . originate new styles in this art."

"For all things' sake," exploded Davis, "Let's go accumulate some background!"

"Yes. At once. F'r sake of all Burkeville, anyhow, best we get this project org'nized fast. Come." She seized his wrist and urged him toward the inner building.

A hesitation came upon Davis. His gaze flickered back to the Councillors. They had taken on avid expressions, but the atmosphere was, somehow, disturbingly unbiological. He cleared his throat.

"But wait a minute, sweetheart. I can understand your, uh, natural curiosity. But have you any plans beyond that?"

" 'Course." Kathleen smiled at him. "We know well enough, we need Men. Watched birds in springtime. Y' give new experience, healthy life, t' whole town."

"Mmmm . . . ye-e-es . . . in the course of time!"

"An' children!" Kathleen's tone grew fierce. "Y' think we like having Doctors boss us? Y'll make us free o' Doctors. We'll have t' hide y', first, play waiting game. But when y'r sons begin t' grow up—un'erstand? We'll own Atlantis!"

Davis' jaw dropped. He backed away. "Wait!" he exclaimed. "Wait just a minute. I thought you'd help me get my own ship back—I could bring all the Men you want . . ."

"An' Burkeville b'comes nothing? No, no, Davis. Here y' stay."

"But . . ."

Kathleen made no signal. None was needed. A dozen warriors stepped from the crowd, into the hall, and leveled their spears.

84

Davis looked about him, wildly. "But my friends!" he stammered.

"Fishbait."

A cold wind sprang up, ruffling the dark lake waters. Barbara wrenched herself from the window. No one was looking her way—they *mustn't* be! She found the ladder and returned to the lake. Swimming slowly for quietness was strain enough to break her.

She swarmed up the rope into the barrack gloom. "Well?" said Valeria.

"Father, Val! Those witches . . . going to keep him here . . . kill us . . . where's my armor?"

Elinor screamed. Barbara cuffed her. "Shut up! Shut up or die!"

The Whitleys began helping each other, lacing corselets above the iron kilts, tugging on boots, strapping down helmets. "Quick!" choked Barbara. "Eclipse is almost over. Elinor, you see that stable across the way? Fetch out four orspers—fresh ones—and . . . yes!" She snatched a brand from the small hearthfire. "Shove this into the straw."

"I, I, I . . ."

Valeria helped her on her way with a lusty kick. "Either that or get your throat slit, my dear," she said.

The westward rim of Minos was turning incandescent when the Whitleys were dressed. They hurried into the street as Elinor shooed four birds through the barn door. No time for saddle or bedroll—but you needed reins, and the fishhead had forgotten that, of course. Barbara darted into the stables. A fire was leaping up in a pile of dry straw. She snatched harness off the wall and ran out.

A Burke child saw them and screamed. The crowd faced slowly around, hampered by its own mass. Barbara slapped a bit into an orsper beak, heard it click home in the notch, threw the crowpiece and front around the stiff blue crest, made the bird crouch, and mounted, tightening the buckle as she did. Elinor wailed. Valeria leaned over. "Harness one for Davis!" she shouted.

Then the Whitleys charged the Burkes.

Father be praised, orspers were stupid enough to turn on their own mistresses, and these had been trained like

85

Freetoon birds. Barbara let beak and claws cut a way for her while she leaned to right and left plying her axe. She didn't know if anyone got killed, didn't care. "Bert! Bert, come out!"

A thrown spear glanced off her cuirass. A saber hewed at her leg, slashing the boot. She cut back and nearly fell off. There was a seething of Burkes; they screamed and tried to run and tripped over each other. The armed women would have held steady, but the mob swirled them away.

Davis appeared. He swung the remnant of a chair and whooped. Part of Barbara's mind said there had never in all the starry universe been so gallant a sight.

Bee drew clear of Minos, full day flooded across the lake. Somehow the Whitleys and Davis were back at the stable. Fire wavered pale in the door, the orspers within screeched. Barbara felt sorry for them, poor birds; she hoped they could be freed, she wished it hadn't been necessary to make them too frantic to ride for a while.

Davis pulled at the crest of a free orsper. It bent down for him and he mounted, a precarious seat without stirrups. Barbara noticed in faint surprise that Elinor was on her own steed—she'd expected the Dyckman to wring her hands till the Burkes chopped her up.

The drawbridge thundered beneath them. There was a road which led from it, westward on the long downgrade to the sea. Dust whirled up from clawed feet and Barbara gave herself to the rocking rhythm of a full-speed run.

The Burkes would put out the fire, she thought bleakly, calm their orspers, and pursue with saddles and spare mounts. She hoped her party had enough of a head start.

CHAPTER XII

Several kilometers from the lake town, Valeria's orsper coughed blood and sank on its breast. "Wounded in the fight," she said bitterly. "I'll double up with Elinor."

"That'll wear her bird out pretty quick," panted Barbara.

"We can switch around," said Valeria.

They resumed at an easier pace. The road was wide and deeply rutted; it must be a trade highway. Forest crowded tall on either side. Already the air was warmer. The trees were hardwood species; midge-like insects glinted in the sun. This land was a steep decline into some great river valley.

"We'd better leave the road as soon as possible," said Barbara.

Davis nodded. "I never . . . I won't say you saved me from a fate worse than death, kid, but I am grateful."

"Maybe now you'll behave yourself," snapped the girl.

Davis shrugged. It almost cost him his seat on the slippery orsper back. He concentrated on staying mounted.

But sunder it! he thought resentfully, it wasn't fair to put him on a planet aswarm with pretty girls and interrupt him every time things began to get interesting. He felt much abused.

His mind turned to the abandoned orsper, dying on a hot dusty road . . . to Burkes, Freetooners, Greendalers maimed and slain, to Barbara and Valeria driven from their home and hunted across high mountains. The situation was unfair to everybody. And Davis Bertram had brought it on.

No court of law would call it his fault. But still, he *had* catalyzed cruelty and murder, and his own blundering had made it worse. Strength, education, a good if somewhat rusty mind gave him the power, and hence the responsibility, to make the crucial decisions. So far he had failed that job.

He got into such a glow of good resolutions that he almost fell off again. It was an effort to ride these birds without a saddle.

Down and down the road wound, snaking about one tumbled vine-grown cliff after another. The low suns blazed in their faces. Now and then they stopped to switch the double weight; otherwise, they continued with the memory of spears at their back. Davis thought that the Burkes would kill him if they couldn't have the exclusive franchise. They were too jealous of their little ingrown society. That was one culture the Service was bound to decide should not be protected.

Meanwhile, though, the orspers neared exhaustion.

Valeria broke a lengthy silence. "It won't do us any good to ride these brutes much longer. It wears us and them out, and the enemy will have spare birds."

"They'll have saddles, too," added Barbara. "We can't fight saddle-mounted riders."

"Better strike out on foot," finished Valeria. "If we can't lose them in these woods they have my permission to barbecue us for breakfast."

"Don't!" Elinor turned slightly green.

"Yeh," said Davis. "I do wish you wouldn't mention food. It's been all day since I ate."

Bee smoldered in coppery sunset clouds. Faintly to their right could be heard the noise of a waterfall. Barbara rubbed her snub nose thoughtfully. "Didn't we pass a trail a kilometer or so back?" she asked.

"Yes . . . little weed-grown bush trail," nodded Davis.

"Well, that means people, and I don't think any people could be very friendly with the Burkes. Especially if you keep your mouth shut, Bert, and act the way a Man ought to."

Ouch!

They rode their orspers off the road, dismounted carefully, and shooed the birds on down the highway. Valeria glided into the forest; Barbara brought up the rear, smoothing out all trace. Thereafter it was a struggle through murky thickets to reach the path.

Minos-light spattered cold between dense leaves. The trail was a tiny one, obviously seldom used, plunging downhill between boulder outcrops and subtropical cane-brakes. There was a heavy smell of green life, growing and rotting; luminous fungi speckled trees nearly choked with vines; the waterfall sound grew louder.

It was a good two hours before they reached the source. Then they emerged on wet stones to see a great river, gunmetal under Minos, leap a full kilometer off a sheer precipice. The king planet grew hazy in a chill mist where dim rainbows danced. The crashing of the waters drowned all voice; human heads rang with it.

The trail, barren and slippery, went down the brink into a canyon. Valeria pointed in that direction. Through the cold foggy light, Davis saw her raise questioning brows, and nodded. She took the lead again, feeling a careful way while rainbowed death roared beside her.

Davis stole a glance at Barbara. The girl was watching the torrent, eyes wide and lips parted. Droplets of mist glimmered like jewels in her hair. His heart gave a thump.

Past midnight, they reached the bottom of the cliff. For a while they rested, watching the whirlpool and the white column of the fall. Then, with a little sigh, Barbara stood up and trudged on.

The trail followed the riverbank. In the brilliant unreal planet glow, Davis saw that the canyon walls spread out ahead of him until they were several kilometers across. But the river widened too, until a sheet of water broad as a lake flowed smoothly between scarps and crags. It occupied nearly the whole canyon floor; this river was as big as the Colorado.

Across a broken shimmer of Minos-light, they could see small rocky islands dotting the surface. Now that they were away from the fall, the air grew warm again. But there wasn't room for forest down here, or even for grass. Poor hunting, if any.

Davis counted up their assets. The girls had their fighting equipment: armor, axes, bows, dirks, lassos looped around the shoulder, hooks and line in their pouches. No bedrolls or frying pan . . . oh, well, they were in a mild climate now.

He and Elinor had nothing but the tattered kilts and the

disintegrating sandals they stood up in.

And my strength, of course. Davis looked complacently at the muscles of his arm. Given the initial distraction of the Whitley attack, he'd had small trouble fighting his way clear of Burke Hall. Kathleen the Second would have a lump on her head to remember him by. *And my education.*

Trouble was, crossbow bolts had small respect for muscle power, and it was no good knowing how to pilot a spaceship and fire a blaster if spaceships and blasters weren't available.

Toward morning, under a rosy eastern sky, Davis made out a really big island ahead of him. It was nearly circular, ten kilometers or so across and thickly overgrown with forest. It came within a few meters of shore, and he thought of swimming out.

Then the down-glow showed him that the place was inaccessible: a giant basaltic outcrop, black cliffs rising ten vertical meters with the woods growing on top. Short of antigrav equipment or magnetronic boots, nobody could . . .

"Hoy!" Valeria came to a halt; stones rattled beneath her feet.

After a moment, Davis saw it too: a slender suspension bridge from the clifftop to the shore. It was anchored by cables of woven vine to a rusty crag on this side, to fronded trees on the island.

Barbara's crossbow clanked into position. "So somebody does live here," she whispered.

"This is where the trail ends," agreed Valeria. "The question is who, and what can we talk them out of?"

Davis felt it incumbent on him to lead the way, though his guts crawled at the thought of a shot. He spoke rapidly, through a dry mouth: "Whoever it is doesn't have to take any nonsense from the Burkes, or anybody except the Doctors. That island must be self-sufficient, and it can't be taken."

"No?" growled Valeria. "I'd beat my way across that bridge alone."

"All they have to do is shoot from the shelter of the woods. And meanwhile they cut those cables. Down comes the bridge. How do you build a new one with the islanders potshotting your engineers?"

"How did they get there in the first place?"

"Ladders, I suppose. Which won't work against any proper defense."

"Mmmm . . . yes. I see." She spoke slowly, as if reluctant to admit he was correct.

Davis halted at the foot of the bridge. There must be someone watching at the other end, in the twilight beneath the trees. He cupped hands around his mouth and bawled: "Hello, up there! We come in peace!"

Echoes clamored between the river and the talus slopes up the canyon wall. There was a brief wait.

Then a slender girl clad in long brown hair and a few flowers stepped to the head of the bridge. She had a crossbow, but didn't aim it at them. "Who are you?" she called timidly.

"She's a Craig," whispered Barbara to Davis. "At home they're all poets and weavers. Now why would a Craig be on sentry-go?"

He paused, drawing himself up impressively. "Know that I am Davis, a Man come from Earth to redeem the old promise," he intoned, feeling rather silly. Barbara smothered a giggle.

"Oh!" The Craig dropped her bow and broke into a tremble. "A Man—*Ohhhh!*"

"I come as the vanguard of all the Men, that they may return to their loyal women and drive evil from the world Atlantis," boomed Davis. "Let me cross your bridge that I may, uh, claim your help in my, er, crusade. Yes, that's it, crusade."

The Craig squeaked and fell on her face. Davis started over the bridge. It was too steep a climb for an impressive march, but the timing was perfect—B just rising in a golden blaze over the waterfall. Barbara and Valeria tramped boldly behind him; even Elinor seemed to regain enough strength to smooth back her tangled hair.

Past the bridge, there was a downward path; the island was cup-shaped. Only the rim of the cup held true forest; elsewhere, the trees grew in orderly groves. The grass beneath them was clipped and there were hedgerows and brilliant flowerbeds.

A few other women emerged from the woods, laying down their bows and axes. They were as sleek, suntanned, and informally dressed as the first one. And their reac-

91

tions were just as satisfactory, a spectrum from abasement to awed gaping.

"More Craigs, couple of Salmons, a Holloway, an O'Brien," murmured Valeria. "Artist, artisan, entertainer and poet classes at home—that sort."

Davis stooped over the first girl and raised her. "You may look on me, my dear," he said unctuously. She herself was worth looking at, too. "I come as your friend."

She dug her toes in the dirt and blushed in various places.

A Holloway, rather big and corpulent, cleared her throat shyly. "We never thought there would be so great an honor for *us*," she whispered. "We thought when the Men came, they'd, er . . ."

Davis puffed himself up. "Do you doubt I am a Man?" he roared.

"Oh, no, ma'am!" The Holloway wrung her hands, cringing from possible thunderbolts. "You're exactly as the songs say, big and beautiful, with a voice like the Leaping Water."

She herself, like the other islanders, had a very pleasing voice. The local accent was a curious blend of exact pronunciation and melodious overtones; they must all have had first-class vocal training. Looking more closely beyond her, Davis saw that the hedges and gardens were arranged with elaborate tastefulness.

But he'd better get his theology straight. "There has been much evil done," he declared, "and to right it, I, the Man, must go as . . . well, as any woman, with only these few loyal attendants. I'm here to summon all women of good will to my cause. The Men help those who help themselves."

"Will you come to our homes, ma'am?"

"The proper form of address is 'sir.' Yes, we will come take rest and refreshment with you, and after that confer with your leaders." Davis beamed and clapped his hands. "Don't . . . I mean, be not afraid. Rejoice!"

"You big chatterbird," hissed Barbara in his ear.

"Shut up," muttered Davis. "I'm having trouble enough keeping a straight face."

The guards needed no more than his consent to start rejoicing. Some dashed ahead, crying out the news, while others ran to pluck flowers and strew them in his path. When he had walked through two kilometers of park-scape, smiling like a politician in a representative-government culture, the whole population came to meet him.

There were about twenty genotypes, he saw, all of the artist-artisan variety. Altogether they numbered about a thousand, including children. They had put on their best clothes, woven dresses, lacy scarfs, feather bonnets, draped leis—the total effect stunned him, a riot of carefully chosen color, flame red and cobalt blue, forest green and hot gold and burnished copper. All bore plain signs of good, easy living; the older women were tremendously fat, the young ones slim and full of grace, with faces and bodies intricately painted.

They danced around him, sang in a choir, reed pipes skirled and a great drum thundered through the woods. Flowers rained on his path and tangled in his hair. Mothers pressed their babies toward him for the touch of his hands. Tame birds with tails like rushing fire strutted on cool grass; whole trees pruned into living statuary rustled overhead; the morning wind went like a benediction across the land.

The village nestled at the bottom of the cup, surprisingly large. But each of the simple grass huts could only have held a few people . . . by Cosmos, here was one place on Atlantis where you had a right to privacy! One long house in the middle of town was of split bamboo-like material, probably used on public occasions. It faced on a green plaza rimmed with cooking pits.

About this time, the past twelve hours caught up with Davis. He managed somehow to inject sufficient pomp into his demand for breakfast and bed. They brought him eggs, fruits, small sweet cakes, and berry wine. Then they conducted him to the chief's house and tucked him into feather bolsters and sang him a lullaby.

Nobody spoke above a whisper all the time he slept.

CHAPTER XIII

Davis awoke near sunset. A girl posted at his bed waved her arm through the curtained door. Others who must have been waiting entered, to kneel with towels and basins of hot water, or stand playing the harp.

"Well, well." Davis yawned enormously. "This is more like it. When do we eat?"

"A feast has been prepared, our unworthy best, if the Man will deign to taste it."

"The Man will deign to make a pig of himself." Davis got out of bed. The floor had been covered with flower petals. The girls were plainly expecting to bathe him, but he chased them out.

An embroidered kilt, a plumed headdress, golden bangles, and a dirk in a tooled-leather scabbard were laid forth for him. He dressed and brushed through the door.

Bee was low between the trees on the island rim; shadows lapped the great bowl, but the air was mild. Women scurried about the roasting pits. When Davis emerged, a crowd of musicians struck up and another band of girls chosen for youth and beauty went out on the green to dance before him.

Valeria stood waiting. She had loosened her red hair, put armor aside in favor of a simple kilt and lei, but the scarred left hand rested on her knife. "Well," she said, "it took you long enough. Nobody would eat before you, and I'm ravenous."

"We seem to have found the kind of place we deserve," said Davis. He started around the plaza toward a dais richly draped with feather cloaks. Barbara lounged by it, in conversation with a Craig who wore the ornaments of leadership and held a carved staff.

"I don't know," said Valeria. "They're friendly enough,

but gutless. This place is so easy to defend, they don't even need a warrior caste—never had one."

"What's it called?"

"Lysum. It's another offshoot of the same conquered town those Burkes ran from. In this case, only a certain class of people got together. They can fish in the river, they have tame fowl, fruits and nuts the year 'round, all the wood and metal they want already stored—they never go anywhere!" Valeria looked disgusted.

Davis felt she was being unjust. Her own rather repulsive virtues, hardihood and fearlessness, would be as redundant here as fangs on a turtle. "How do they spend their time, then?" he asked.

"Oh, they do what little work there is, and the rest of it goes to arts, poetry, craft, music, flowers . . . Yah!"

Glancing at the delicately carved wood, subtly designed ornament, intricate figure dances, listening to choral music which was genuinely excellent, Davis got fed up with Valeria. Nobody had a right to be so narrow-minded. Here on Lysum they seemed as free as in Burkeville—no, infinitely more so; there wasn't the deadening monotony of a single genotype. Eventually, no doubt, this culture would stagnate if left to itself—but today it was young, creative, and happy.

The Craig on the dais stood up for him. She was not old enough to be fat; given a stronger chin she would have been quite pretty . . . though Barbara, in kilt and lei, was unfair competition. "Be welcome among us, Man." Now that the first shock had worn off, the Craig spoke with confidence. "Atlantis has never known a happier day than this—oh, we're so *thrilled!* All Lysum is yours."

"Thanks." Davis sat down, and she lowered herself to the ground before him. "You are the leader here?"

"Yes, sir. Yvonne Craig, Prezden of Lysum, your servant."

Davis looked around. "Where's Elinor?"

"Still pounding her ear, of course," snorted Barbara. "Want to wait for her?"

"Cosmos, no! When do we—I mean, Prezden Yvonne, let the banquet begin!"

Horns blew, the dance ended, the women of Lysum hurried to their places. Rank seemed strictly according to age, the oldest seated on the ground nearest Davis—which was a pity, in a way, though it was pleasant to see a casteless society. The children began serving at once, and that was a relief.

The food was delicious; the first cuisine he had encountered on Atlantis. And the courses went on and on, and the wooden winebowls were kept filled.

Sundown smoldered across the sky. Theseus, half full, came from behind Minos to add his ruddy light; stars powdered a velvety heaven and a warm breeze flowed down from the island rim with a smell of spices. Davis ate onward.

Music was played, but nobody spoke. He leaned toward Yvonne. "I am pleased with what I have seen here," he told her.

"You are *so* sweet . . . I mean, gracious," she thrilled happily.

"Elsewhere there's devilment on the loose. The will of the Men is for peace among all, but first the wrongdoers must be punished."

"Your serving woman"—that got a scowl from Barbara and a snicker from Valeria—"told me that the Burkes had dared set on you with force."

"Ah, yes. You know the Burkes of Burkeville, then?"

"Slightly, sir. Nasty folk! Really, I don't know what the world is coming to. Why can't people leave each other in peace?" Yvonne had drunk a bit more than was wise—so had everybody—and spoke fast. *"Honestly,* sir, you wouldn't *believe* what some of those towns are like! Thank Father we don't have to have much to do with them. They're just *vile!"*

The Whitleys flanked Davis on the seat. Valeria leaned over and whispered: "See what I mean? No help here. I told this featherbelly we'd want some spears to follow us, and she near fainted."

"Mmmm . . . yes." Davis felt a moment's grimness. He couldn't look for armed assistance from Lysum—if offered, it would be rather less than no good—and he couldn't stay holed up here forever. No wonder Val was so down on the islanders; she was more disappointed than intolerant. Not a bad girl, Val, in her waspish way. Davis tilted his winebowl. His free arm stole about Barbara's waist. She regarded him mistily.

"Strong, this drink," she said. "Wha's it called?"

"A jug of wine, and thou," smiled Davis.

"Bubbles in my head . . ." Barbara leaned against him.

"Oh, here comes dessert," said Yvonne.

Davis could barely wrap himself around the elaborate confection.

The Prezden gave him a large-eyed look. Minos-light streamed over sprawling feminine forms. "Will you require us all tonight, sir?" she asked interestedly.

"Yipe!" said Davis.

"Go ahead." Valeria's low tone was surly. "I don't suppose it'll hurt matters here."

"Like hell you will!" Barbara opened her eyes, sat straight up, and glared at him.

Yvonne looked bewildered. Barbara was quite tight enough to start an argument, and that would never do. Davis donned a somewhat boozy benevolence.

"I thank you," he said. "It would not be fitting, though. Tonight I must, urp, think on weighty problems. I would be alone."

Yvonne bent her long-tressed head. "As the Man wishes. My house is his." Her dignity collapsed in a titter. "I am his too, if he changes his mind. Or any of us would be so *thrilled*—"

Sunblaze! thought Davis. This was too good a chance to miss. What had gotten into Barbara, anyhow? She sat brooding at Minos, nearly on the point of tears. Too much wine, no doubt.

Yvonne stood up and clapped her hands. "The Man wishes to be alone tonight," she called. "All you girls scat!"

In five minutes the door curtains had closed on the last islander. Davis gaped. It was not what he had meant.

Valeria got to her feet, put an arm under Barbara's shoulders. "I'll see her to bed," she said coldly. "Goodnight."

"Oh, no, you don't," said Davis. "Run along yourself. Babs and I have a little matter to discuss of who's boss here."

Valeria grinned. "Care to stop me . . . Man?"

Davis watched them disappear into one of the huts.

"Death and destruction!" he said gloomily, and poured himself another drink.

He was tipsy, but there was no sleep in him. Presently he wandered off across a sward glistening with dew, under the light-spattered shade of high trees.

The fact is, and we might as well face it with our usual modesty, Barbara is in love with me. Maybe she doesn't quite realize it yet, but I know the symptoms. Well?

Davis realized he was a little scared . . . not of her, he decided after cogitating for a while, but of the consequences to himself. From time to time, there had been such girls, and he'd run like a jackrabbit. He didn't want to be tied down yet!

He climbed the long slope until he stood on the island rim and looked across the swirling darkness of the river. It murmured and chuckled beneath him, around him, the light of Minos and two moons and the few stars not drowned out shivered and broke on the surface; he saw foam where a rock jutted upward.

He stood for a time, watching. After all, he wasn't important; nobody was, in this broken wilderness of stone and water and moonlight. He couldn't just walk away from Barbara; he needed her for a guide if nothing else. But he wasn't so almighty wonderful that she couldn't forget him as soon as some other spacemen arrived.

If she got mad at him, he thought woozily, it would help her over the infatuation. And what would make her mad at him? Why, jealousy would do it. A Man had every right to change his mind; it wouldn't disillusion Lysum if he . . . Yes, they were disappointed in him already; he'd better remedy that situation at once.

He started quickly back toward the village. Let's see, now, protocol doubtless made Yvonne the candidate for tonight . . . uh, which hut was she using now?

He came out of a grove, with the valley open before him down to the darkened houses, and stopped. There was a tall form approaching. "Barbara," he said numbly.

She came to him, smiling and shaking the loose red hair down over her back, but her eyes were big, solemn, a little afraid. "Bert," she whispered. "I wanted to talk to you."

She had no right to be so beautiful. Davis choked. She halted and stood with hands clasped behind her back, like a child. It was the only childlike thing about her, as Minos made abundantly clear.

"Um . . . sure . . . you got rid of that spitcat cousin of yours, I see," he began feebly.

"She's asleep. I wanted this to be between us two."

"Oh, yes, of course. Can't settle anything with Valeria sticking her nose into the business. Ask her a civil question and you get a civil war."

"Val . . . oh." The girl looked away. Light and shadow flowed across her. Suddenly she swung her head back to him. "What do you have against Valeria?"

"What does she have against me?" he shrugged. "She's a natural born shrew, I suppose."

"She means well. It's just that she . . . never quite knows what to say . . . and she's afraid of you."

"Afraid!" Davis laughed.

"I know her. We *are* of the same blood. Can't you . . ."

"Scuttle Valeria!" said Davis thickly. "Come here, you."

She crept into his arms, her hands stole from behind her back and closed around his neck. He kissed her, taking his time and savoring it . . . Her response had an endearing clumsiness.

She laid her face against his breast. "I couldn't stand it, Bertie," she confessed. "You and all those other women . . ."

"When you put it that way, every other woman in the Galaxy goes out of existence for me," said Davis.

She looked up again; the cool gold light glimmered off tears. "Do you mean that?"

"Of course I do," said Davis, concluding that he was sincere after all.. At least, he was ready to forego everybody in Lysum if . . .

"I was so afraid," she said brokenly. "I didn't know what was happening to me, I thought I was psyched."

"Poor little Babs." He stroked her hair. "Sit down."

They spent a while without words. He was delighted to see how fast she learned.

"I was always alone," she said at last. "I had to be, don't you understand? It was hard for me to admit to myself . . . that I could belong to anyone else . . ."

Touched, he kissed her more gently. They were in the

99

shadow of a frondtree; he could scarcely see her save as a warm breathing shape next to him.

She waited a little, as if gathering courage, then said: "Do whatever you want to, Bert."

Davis reached for her—and pulled up cold.

It was one thing to make love to an Elinor, a Kathleen, an Yvonne. Barbara was a different case entirely. He couldn't just run off and leave *her;* he had to live with himself. He wasn't that kind of scoundrel; she was too whole-hearted, it would hurt her too much when he finally left.

At the same time, he wasn't going to humiliate her into storming off. That had been the plan, half an hour ago, but conditions were changed. He needed time to decide what he really wanted.

"Well?" she asked.

"Well, this is a serious matter," said Davis. "You'd better think it over for a while."

"I've thought it over for days, darling."

"Yes, but . . ."

"But nothing! Come here." Small calloused hands closed on his wrists.

Davis talked. And talked. And talked. He wasn't sure what he said, but it included words like sanctity. At the end, with sweat running down his ribs, he asked if she understood.

"No," she sighed. "But I suppose you know best."

"I wonder—never mind! Of course I do."

"It's really been enough, to be here with you. There'll be other times. Whenever you want to . . ."

"Cut that out!" groaned Davis. "Give me a kiss and go to bed."

She gave him a long one. Then, rising: "There is one thing, my beloved. The others in our party . . ."

"Mmmm, yes. I can handle Elinor, but I hate to think what Val would say."

"Don't let on to anyone. Not to me or . . . only when we're alone."

"All right. That does make it easier. Run along, sweetheart. I want to think."

"With the Craig?" she asked coldly.

"Cosmos, no!"

"I'll kill you if you do. I mean it."

"Yes," he muttered, "I'll take your word for that."

"Goodnight, Bertie. I care for you."

"The word," he said, "is love."

"I love you, then." She laughed, with a little sob, and sped down the hill.

Davis rose to his feet, not unpleasantly stunned. She ran like a deer, he thought—why couldn't she be trained for spatial survey? Married teams were common enough . . .

The girl stumbled. She spread her hands, regained balance, and continued.

Davis felt the wind go out of him. There had been a scar on her left hand.

CHAPTER XIV

Barbara woke up and wished she hadn't.

There were hammers behind her eyes, and she was abominably thirsty. A jug of water stood by her bed. She poured herself a long draught. At once the planet waltzed around her.

She grabbed her head and reeled off a string of cavalry oaths. The young O'Brien who peered in blushed. "Does my lady want anything?" she asked shyly.

"Don't shout at me!" snarled Barbara. "What the fire and thunder did you feed me last night?"

"Only the banquet, my lady, and the wine— Oh. I see. If my lady will permit . . ." The O'Brien scuttled out again.

Barbara rolled over on her stomach and buried her face in her hands. Foggy recollections came back; yes, Val had helped her to bed and then she passed out . . . Davis making eyes at that Yvonne trollop . . . Father!

The O'Brien came back with a bowl of herb tea. It helped. Breakfast followed, and life was merely desolate. Barbara tottered out into the open.

It was a little past eclipse. The islanders were going about their usual business in their usual leisurely fashion. Prezden Yvonne ran warbling to greet her, received a bloodshot glare, and backed off. Barbara smoldered her way toward a fruit grove.

Valeria came into sight, wringing out her hair and glistening with wetness. "Oh, hello, small one," she grinned. "I recommend a swim. The water's wonderful."

"What have you got to be so happy about?"

Valeria did a few steps of the soldier's axe dance. "Beautiful, beautiful, beautiful day," she caroled. "I *love* this place!"

"Then it's too bad we're getting out of here."

"Whatever for?"

"What reason is there to stay? So that Davis can make

up to all the women on Lysum?" Barbara kicked miserably at the turf. "I imagine he's still sleeping it off."

"Well, he did get to bed quite late, poor dear," said her twin. "But he was just walking around, thinking."

Barbara started. "How do you know?"

Valeria flushed. "I couldn't sleep. I sat up and watched till nearly Bee-rise."

"Then you ought to be snoring yet."

"Don't need sleep." Valeria jumped after a red fruit, seized it, and crunched it between small white teeth. "Look, Babs, we're not in your kind of hurry. We need a rest, and this is the place to take it. Also, we'll have to get orspers . . . negotiate with some other town; they don't have 'em here . . ."

"I thought you knew. One of the local yuts told me yesterday. This river runs straight down to the sea, and that waterfall behind us is the last one. They have boats here. We'll commandeer one and make the trip twice as fast. That's how the Lysumites go to the Ship. They buy passage from the seafolk and . . ."

"Oh, hell, Babs." Valeria laid a hand on her shoulder. "We have a fair chance of getting killed somewhere along the way, and life's too good to waste. Let's take a few days off, at least."

"What's got into you, anyway?" Barbara narrowed her eyes.

Valeria didn't answer, but strolled down the slope toward the village.

Barbara drifted glumly in the opposite direction. Her cousin's advice was hard to refute, but she didn't like it. This place was just sickly sweet. That Yvonne—ugh!

She passed the guards at the bridge, ignoring their respects, and walked across to the shore. The water did look clean and cool. She peeled off her clothes and waded moodily out.

The swim helped. Seated again on the rocky bank, she found her head clear enough to hold the problem. Which was that she wanted Davis for herself.

Just what that would mean, she wasn't sure, but the thought made heat and cold chase each other through her skin. There was his funny slow smile, and his songs, and his gentleness . . .

103

Then the thing to do was tell Davis. Tonight, when everybody was asleep, she'd sneak out and find him and . . . Somehow, the thought made her giddy. But to know where she stood and what she meant to do about it was like a fresh cup of that what-you-call-it drink. And maybe just as treacherous, but you couldn't stay alive without taking risks.

She put her kilt back on and returned almost merrily.

Elinor was in front of the Big House chatting to a Holloway. "Oh, my dear, you wouldn't believe it, it is simply *awful* up on the pass, I honestly thought I would freeze to death, and you know I was used to *much* better things in Freetoon, I was really quite impor— Oh, Barbara."

The Whitley felt such an all-embracing benevolence that it even included Dyckmans. "Hello, dear," she smiled, and stroked the other girl's hair. "You're looking lovely." She nodded and drifted on.

"Well!" said Elinor. "Well, I never! After the way she treated me, to come greasing up like . . . Prudence, darling, let me tell you . . ."

Davis emerged from the Prezdon's hut. He looked wretched. Barbara's heart turned over with pity. She ran toward him calling his dear name and wondered why he jerked.

"Bert, what's the matter? It's such a beautiful day. Don't you feel well?"

"No," said Davis hollowly.

Valeria joined them. Barbara had never seen her cousin walk in that undulant fashion—why, she might almost have been a Dyckman. Was everybody falling sick?

Davis started. "Lemme out of here," he muttered.

Valeria's cheeks flamed. "Hello," she said. Her tone was not quite as cool as usual.

"Gwmpf," said Davis, backing away.

Barbara took his arm and looked reproachfully at Valeria. "It's such a shame you two don't get along," she said. "We've been through so much together."

Valeria drew her knife and tested its edge with her thumb. Davis turned green and disengaged himself from Barbara.

"I don't feel so good," he said in a ramshackle voice.

"Let me alone for a while, you two, please."

As he wobbled away, Barbara turned on her twin in a rage. "Will you keep your paws off my business?"

"What business?" Valeria tossed the knife up and caught it.

"When I have private matters to talk over with him, I don't want you around!"

"Oh . . . so that's it?" Valeria stood for a while in thought. "I'd hoped you would have enough decency to stay in your hut at night."

"Just because you're a dull fish with a clinker for a heart . . ."

"In fact," began Valeria, "I must insist, Babs, that . . ."

The musical winding of a horn interrupted her.

Both Whitleys felt their sinews tauten. "From the bridge," said Barbara through stiff lips. "Somebody's coming."

"It may not mean anything," answered Valeria. "But let's not take chances. We'd better keep out of sight. You collect Elinor, I'll fetch Bert. Meet you in that tanglewood stand up on the rim."

Barbara nodded and ran off. Elinor, stretching langorously before the burly Holloway, was suddenly yanked off her feet. "Come along," said Barbara.

"What do you mean, you . . . you *creature?*"

"Jump." A drawn dagger gleamed across the sky. Elinor jumped.

Valeria guided Davis after them. Oddly, he seemed almost relieved by the prospect of action. They entered the copse and looked from its concealment toward the bridge path.

"Everybody's seen us come up here," said Davis. "If it's an enemy . . ."

". . . we can jump off the cliff and swim to the boat dock," said Barbara. Her veins pulsed.

Elinor closed her eyes and swooned toward Davis. He stepped aside and she hit the ground with an outraged squawk.

There was a bustle down in the village; its people leaped to form ceremonial ranks. A troop of guards emerged from the park. A veiled woman on orsperback, leading four other birds, jogged solemnly after.

"Father!" whispered Valeria. "It's a legate!"

"A what?" asked Davis.

"Messenger from the Doctors. What does she want?"

Barbara peered between the branches, and the awe of eight years ago rose within her. That had been the last time a legate was in Freetoon. There had been a crop failure, and she had come to adjust the payment of annual tribute.

She was tall, unidentifiable under the long travel-stained gown of white, hooded blue cloak, trousers and gold-chased boots, heavy veil. One of the extra orspers bore a pack, the others were merely saddled. As the legate dismounted, Yvonne prostrated herself.

Valeria snapped her fingers. "I think I have it," she said excitedly. "Remember, we sent our fastest couriers from Freetoon to the Ship when Bert first arrived. They must have gotten there a couple of weeks ago. Now the Doctors are sending to every town . . . word about the Man . . ."

"Wait a minute," said Davis. "The Ship is a long way off. Nobody could get here so soon."

"A legate could," Barbara told him. "They can requisition anything they want—food, orspers, guides—and they're trained to ride for days and nights at a stretch."

"Well," said Davis. "Well, this is terrific! Our troubles are over, girls. Let's go see her."

"Not just yet," muttered Barbara. "She'll send for us when we're wanted."

"Yeh?" Davis bristled. "Who does she think she is?"

"I know, I know," said Valeria. "But why give offense?"

Davis shrugged. "As you will."

The veiled woman entered the Big House. Her baggage was removed and brought in after her, then she was alone. A party of girls ran up the slope.

"Man! Man, you're wanted—the legate wants to see you!"

Davis smiled importantly and stepped out of the thicket. The Whitleys followed, ignoring the chatter of everyone else.

106

They came down to the plaza. Yvonne, throwing on her best feather bonnet, laid a finger across her lips. "Shhhh!"

"I want to see the legate," said Davis.

"Yes, sir, yes . . . she'll come when she's ready . . . just wait here."

Davis went to the dais.

"Oh, you mustn't sit, sir!" Yvonne tugged at his arm. "Not when the legate is here!"

Davis gave her a frosty stare. "For your information," he said, "a Man ranks a legate by six places."

Yvonne looked unhappy.

Stillness lay thick over the island. The Lysumites huddled together, watching Davis and the Big House with frightened eyes. Barbara and Valeria joined him, but dared not be seated. Elinor squeezed next to the Prezden and shivered.

There was a half hour's wait. Davis yawned, stretched, scratched himself, and looked increasingly mutinous. Barbara grew afraid of what the legate might think.

She stiffened herself. He was her Man, and she would fight the whole Ship for him if she had to!

Father did not strike her dead. She felt a sense of triumph, as if the fact were a personal victory.

Nevertheless, when the legate emerged her knees bumped together.

The woman had changed into full ceremonials. A robe of green fell sheer to her feet, a gloved hand gripped a long staff of some unknown shimmery metal, a plumed mask in the shape of an orsper head covered her own and made it coldly unhuman.

Davis got up. "Hello, ma'am," he smiled.

The tall woman did not stir. She stood a few meters away from him, alien in the long sunbeams, and waited. Sweat glistened on Valeria's forehead; Barbara felt it on her own. She stood rigid, as if on parade.

Davis said, "I am the Man. You, uh, you know about me?"

"Yes," said the legate. She had a low voice, curiously distorted by the mask, and a stiff accent.

"You've, ahem, come about me?"

"Yes. The Ship and all Atlantis have awaited the Men

107

for three hundred years. How many of you are there?"

"I came by myself. Otherwise no one would have done so for a long time yet."

"Will others follow you?"

"Sure. If I go back and tell them about this place, there'll be Men all over it."

"But otherwise not?"

"I don't know how much you know of the situation . . ." Davis stepped toward her.

"Word came from Freetoon that a ship had landed with someone aboard who might be a Man. Legates have been sent everywhere to inquire if there were others. How did you get here, so far from Freetoon . . . did you fly?"

"Well, no." Davis cleared his throat. "You see, there was a, a misunderstanding. Four other towns allied themselves against Freetoon to capture me and my ship. They overcame us. Being weaponless, I got away with three friends. We were going to the Doctors, to request their assistance in getting my ship back."

The voice remained altogether emotionless; it wasn't *human,* thought Barbara with a chill, to greet this news that way. "But the allied towns cannot use your ship, can they?"

"Oh, no. Can't even get into it. Not without me." Davis came closer, smiling all over his face. "They'll give it up again, on your orders, and I'll go fetch all the Men you want."

"It was a risk," said the legate calmly. "If you had died on this journey, there would be no Men coming after you."

"True," said Davis. "I'm an explorer, you see, and the Galaxy is so big . . ." He preened himself. Barbara thought he looked much too smug, but it was lovable just the same.

"Have you any weapons?" asked the legate.

"No, I told you. Only this dirk here . . . but . . ."

"I understand."

The legate strode from him, toward the bridge guards who stood holding their bows in what Barbara considered a miserable approximation of dress parade. Her voice rang out:

"This is no Man, it's a Monster. Kill it!"

CHAPTER XV

For a moment nobody stirred.

The legate whirled on Yvonne. "I order you in the name of Father," she yelled. "Kill the filthy thing!"

Davis spread his hands, stunned into helplessness. The women of Lysum wailed; a baby burst into tears; Elinor Dyckman shrieked.

Barbara had no time to think. She jumped, snatched a bow from a half paralyzed guard, and lifted it to her shoulder. "The first one of you to move gets a bolt through the belly," she announced.

Valeria's dagger flared directly before the legate. "And this witch gets a slit throat," she added. "Hold still, you!"

In Freetoon the arbalests would have been snapping already. But these were a timid folk who had not known battle for generations. "Drop your weapons," said Barbara. She swiveled her own from guard to guard as she backed toward the house. "Quick! No, you don't!" She fired, and the Salmon who had raised a bow dropped it, stared stupidly at a skewered hand, and fainted. "Next time I aim for the heart," said Barbara.

Weapons clattered to the grass. There went a moan through the densely packed crowd.

Davis shook a benumbed head. "What's the matter?" he croaked. "I *am* a Man. Give me a chance to prove it . . ."

"You have proved it," shouted the legate. "Proved yourself a Monster when you assaulted the Ship's own envoy. Prezden, do your duty!"

Yvonne Craig shuddered her way backward, lifting helpless hands. "You mustn't," she whimpered. "You can't . . ."

"Can't we just?" leered Valeria. She flourished her dagger across the long green robe. "Behave yourself, or Lysum becomes the first town in the world where a legate was stabbed."

To the masked woman: "What's the meaning of this?"

"Barren will you be," said the legate, "and outlaw on Atlantis."

Barbara looked through a haze of terror at Davis. Surely the Man could override such a curse!

He shook himself, and spoke swiftly: "Unless you want to die, lady, you'd better tell these people to obey us."

Valeria emphasized the request with another flourish. Malevolence answered Davis: "So be it, then . . . for now! Don't think you'll escape Father."

Davis turned to the Whitleys. He was pale and breathed hard, but the words rattled from him: "We have to get out of here. Keep these people covered. I'll take charge. You, you, you, you . . ." His fingers chose young, horror smitten girls. "Fetch out all our stuff. And the legate's pack. You over there, I want food, plenty of it. Bread, fruits, fowl, dried fish. Bundle it up!"

Yvonne sank to her knees, and covered her face. "Excuse us, lady," she whimpered. "We'll do what you say . . . anything . . ."

"Let them have their way for now," said the legate coolly. "Father isn't ready yet to strike them down."

"Pick up some bows, Elinor," said Davis.

"No . . . no, you Monster . . ." she gasped.

"Suit yourself," he laughed harshly. "Stay here if you want to be torn to pieces as soon as we're gone."

Shaking, she collected an armful of weapons.

The girls came out with their bundles. "Here, give me an axe," said Davis. "We're going. Babs, Val, cover our rear . . . make everybody follow at a distance so we can't be shot from the woods. I'll watch the dear legate."

Barbara obeyed in a mechanical fashion. Her mind was still gluey; she didn't know if she could move any more without him to think for her.

They went up the path, a scared and sullen village trailing them several meters behind and staring into the Whitley bowsights. Davis told the women to stop at the bridgehead, took his own party across, then cut the cables with a few hard axe strokes. The bridge collapsed into the water and broke up.

"How do we get back?" cried a young Holloway.

"Are you going to eat us?" shivered a Craig.

"Not if you behave yourselves," Davis told her. "As for getting back, you can swim out and let 'em lower ropes for you. I just don't want word of this to get out for a while, and it'll take a couple of weeks at least to rebuild a bridge that orspers can cross. Now, take us to those boats I heard somebody mention."

The burdened women led the way along the shale bank. Yvonne stood on the cliffs and howled loyal curses. Valeria faced around when they were out of bowshot and said slowly, "Bert, I never thought you would be so . . ."

"This kind of situation I can handle," he said.

Barbara's tautness melted as she looked at him. Physical courage was cheap enough, especially when you were desperate, she thought, but he was being as swift with decision as an Udall . . . and ever so much nicer.

A bluff jutted into the river ahead of them, screening a small inlet where the Lysumites had built their dock. A score of long slim bark canoes with carved stemposts were drawn up on the land. Davis told his prisoners to load one. "And set the others afire," he added to Barbara. "Too bad, but we've got to bottle up the word of this till we can get clear."

She nodded, and took forth tinder and fire piston from her pouch. Flame licked across the hulls, and the girls of Lysum wept.

"All right," Davis selected paddles and patching materials. "Now we tie up our guest and get started. Scram, you females. Boo!" He waved his arms, and the youngsters fled a flurry of screams.

Barbara took a certain satisfaction in binding the legate's wrists and ankles and tossing her among the supplies. Elinor huddled near the captive; big help she'd be unless they could extract her knowledge of the Ship . . . but a rattlepate like her wouldn't have noticed anything useful . . . They shoved the canoe into deeper water and climbed aboard.

"Ever used a boat like this?" asked Davis. "No? Well, you'll get the trick soon enough. We'd better paddle two at

111

a time . . . Val, you get in the bow, Babs take the stern. Elinor and I will spell you; I can make up for her, I suppose. Now, then, you kneel, hold your paddle like so . . ."

The current was fast in midstream. Barbara fell quickly into the rhythm of paddling; it wasn't such hard work, though you had to beware of rocks.

Ariadne rose above Ay-set, and Theseus was already up. It would be a bright night. Barbara could have wished for clouds, she felt so exposed under the naked sky; there was a blotch on Minos like a great bloodshot eye glaring down at her.

No, she told herself, Father was a lie . . . at least, the stiff lightning-tossing Father of the Ship did not exist; or if he did, then Bert with his long legs and blue eyes and tawny beard was a stronger god. Merely looking at him made her want to cry.

He grinned into her gaze and wiped sweat off his face. "I don't want to go through that again!" he said. "It'll take a week for me to uncoil."

Valeria looked over her shoulder. "But we got away," she whispered. "Thanks to you, we got away."

"To me? Thunderation! If you two hadn't . . . Well, the problem now is, what do we do next?"

What indeed? thought Barbara. A Man and three women . . . two and a half women . . . with every hand on Atlantis against them . . . But he would think of something. She just knew he would.

Davis regarded the legate thoughtfully where she lay. "I wonder what's beneath that fancy helmet," he murmured. "Let's see."

"You'll fry for this!" she spat.

"Don't," wailed Elinor.

"Shut up." Davis leaned over and lifted the gilt orsper head. Barbara, who had half expected haloes or some such item, was almost disappointed when the ash-blonde hair, cut short, and coldly regular features of a Trevor appeared.

Elinor covered her eyes and crouched shuddering. "I d-d-didn't want to see, ma'am," she pleaded.

"You've fallen into bad company, child," said the

112

Trevor. Then, to Davis: "Are you satisfied, Monster?"

"No." He ran a hand through unkempt yellow hair. "What have you got against me? Don't you know I'm a Man? You must have *some* biological knowledge to operate that parthenogenetic wingding."

"You aren't a Man. You can't be. It isn't possible." The Trevor lay back, scowling in the light that spilled from the sky. "There is a certain sign by which the Men shall be known . . ."

"What sign? Quick!"

"It's a holy secret," she snapped.

"You mean you can't think of anything," said Davis. "And even at Freetoon, where they also doubted I was a Man, they didn't want me murdered out of hand."

After a moment, he went on, almost to himself: "It's a common enough pattern in history. You Doctors have had it soft for three hundred years—two hundred, anyway, once these people had gotten scattered and ignorant enough for the present system to grow up. You must always have dreaded the day when the Men would finally arrive and upset your little wagon. When I told you— foolish of me, but how was I to know?—when I told you I'm alone and there won't be any others for a long time if I don't return—well, your bosses at the Ship must already have told you what to do if that was the case."

"You're a Monster!" said the Trevor. Dogmatic as ever.

"Even if you honestly thought I was, you wouldn't have told them to cut me down. Even a Monster could go home and call the true Men. No, no, my friend, you're a pretty sophisticated lot at the Ship, and you've already decided to rub out the competition."

"Be still before Father strikes you dead!"

Davis grinned. He let her squirm for a while. "Not quite so much twisting, if you please," he said. "A canoe is easy to upset. We can all swim ashore, but you're hogtied."

The Trevor grew rigid.

Davis nodded and looked at Barbara. "Legates sent to every town on this continent," he said. "Orders to learn what the facts are. You'll dicker with the Men if there really are a lot of them or if they can call for help—otherwise kill them and deny everything."

"I'd like to kill *her*," said Barbara between her teeth.

"You Whitleys always were a Fatherless lot," said the Trevor.

"How do you know?" snapped Davis. "Babs, have you any idea who the Doctors are . . . how many, what families?"

"I'm not sure." She frowned, trying to remember. A child always picked up scraps of information meant only for initiates . . . she overheard this, was blabbed that by a garrulous helot—"There are a few thousand of them, I believe. And they're said to be of the best families."

"Uh-huh. I thought so. Inferior types couldn't maintain this system. Even with that tremendous advantage of theirs—that the next generation depends on them —there'd have been more conflict between Church and States unless . . . Yeh, Trevors, Whitleys, Burkes, that sort—the high castes of Freetoon, with the wits and courage and personality to override any local chief — Well."

Barbara shoved her paddle through murmurous waters. The boat moved swiftly. The canyon walls were already lower on either side, a Minos-drenched desolation.

"But what are we going to do?" she asked in helplessness.

"I think—yes. I really think we can get away with it. How long'll it take us to reach a place where they have warriors?"

"That girl I spoke to on the island said it was about ten days by canoe to the sea, and the sea people have a base there."

"Good! Nobody will be off Lysum by that time."

"*I* would skin down a rope and hike after help," said Valeria.

"*They* won't. You know what they're like. Or even if they do, the word will still be far behind us when we get to the coast." Davis took a long breath. "Now, then. Either of you two is about the size of this dame. You can pass for a legate yourself . . ."

Barbara choked. After a moment, Valeria shook her head. "No, Bert. It can't be done. Every child in the soldier families gets that idea as soon as she can talk . . . why not pass a Freetoon Whitley off as a Greendaler? There

114

are countersigns and passwords to prevent just that."

"I'm not surprised," said Davis. "But it isn't what I meant. Look here. We won't try to get into the Ship, but one of you will wear this robe and mask. How are the sea people to know you're not a genuine legate, bringing back a genuine Man? Only, on his behalf, you requisition an escort and a lot of fast orspers. We ride back to Freetoon, demand my own boat—oh, yes, our tame legate can also order your town set free. Then we all hop into my spaceship and ride to Nerthus—and return with a thousand armed Men!"

Barbara thought dazedly that only he could have forged such a plan.

CHAPTER XVI

Eight Atlantean days later, the canoe nosed into Shield Skerry harbor.

The tides on this world varied with the position of the other moons, but they were always enormous—up to seven times the corresponding rise on Earth. A tidal bore here amounted to a virtual tsunami. Except for the frequent case of sheer cliffs, the continents had no definite shorelines, only salt marshes that faded into the ocean. Two hundred kilometers away, the river grew brackish; another hundred kilometers and its estuary was lost in the swamps.

That was a weird gray land, shifting hourly between flood and drenched muckflats; seabirds filling the air with wings and harsh screams as they looked for stranded fish, and always a damp wind out of the west, smelling of kelpish decay. The local life had adapted. Trees lifted gloomily above high tide; ebb showed amphibious grass in queasy hummocks; flippered relatives of the lake monster cawed from their rookeries. It would have been a thirsty trip, blundering lost through a brine-drenched wilderness, had the swampfolk not met them.

There were a few women who lived here, building their miserable huts on whatever high ground existed, gliding in pirogues to hunt and fish, catching rainwater in crude cisterns. They were the weaker and duller families, the servile class of Freetoon, who had colonized a country no one else wanted, and they had fallen to a naked neolithic stage of tomtom rites and bones through the nose. But they were inoffensive enough, specialists in guiding parties between the sea-dweller base and the upper valley. It earned them a few trade goods.

Valeria, impressive in veil and robe, simply commandeered help. A few husky Nicholsons at the paddles made the canoe move like greased lightning. Meanwhile Barbara sat next to the Trevor with a knife in her hand and a sweet smile on her face.

Several days earlier, Valeria had suggested cutting their prisoner's throat, but Davis wouldn't have it.

"Why not?" asked Valeria. "Perfectly normal precaution. She's only a dangerous nuisance."

"Well, it just isn't done. Cosmos! It'll take the psychotechs a hundred years to fit you hellcats into civilization." Davis searched for a reason she would understand. "We may find some use for her yet . . . information, hostage . . ."

Valeria shrugged doubtfully. But neither of the cousins was disposed to argue with their Man.

The lack of privacy and the weariness of incessant paddling, watch and watch, was a blessing, thought Davis. It staved off his own problem. The notion that someday he'd face it again—maybe alone in space with two jealous Whitleys, because he couldn't leave them defenseless against the Doctors' revenge—made his nerves curl up and quiver at the ends.

Not that it had seemed such a bad idea at first. He had even toyed with thoughts of bigamy. Now that he had gained some insight about Valeria, he found her no different from her twin. They were both spitcats, yes, but a man could soon learn to handle them. He couldn't think of two girls he would rather learn to handle. As far as civilized law was concerned, and even custom on most planets, his sex life was his own business. . . .

Inspired by the beautiful logical simplicity of it all, he decided one afternoon to lead up to the suggestion. He was off duty, resting near the bow while the canoe glided between forested riverbanks. Elinor and the Trevor were asleep; Valeria knelt in the stern, driving her paddle in the same powerful rhythm as her sister.

Davis looked from one Whitley to another. Sunlight spilled over ruddy hair. Their bare brown skins glistened with sweat. Each time the paddles bit water, muscles stood forth on Barbara's back and Valeria's belly, and their breasts rose and fell. He got to his own knees, just behind Barbara, and leaned close. The warm sweet smell

117

of her was a drunkenness; his temples pounded. "Babs," he husked.

She turned her face just enough for him to see how smooth her cheek was. "Yes?" Her answer was low and not entirely steady.

"I wanted to say . . . I'm sorry I got you into all this—"

"You didn't," she breathed. "And even if you did, I'm not sorry. Not as long as you're in the same mess."

"After this is all over . . . could we maybe—the three of us—keep on messing around?"

He realized later she must not have noticed that detail of 'three.' She murmured, "I'd adore to." He cupped her breasts in his hands. She leaned back against him, shivering.

A knife thunked into the wood beside them. Valeria's hurled paddle bounced off Davis' head. "Get away from him, you goldbricking slime worm!" she yelled.

Barbara whipped about, drawing her own knife. "Who do you think you are, telling me what to do?"

The canoe had nearly capsized before Davis restored peace. Thereafter he abandoned all notion of a *ménage à trois,* postponed the unsolvable problem of choosing one of them, and concentrated on immediate matters.

He tried to quiz the legate. Beyond the information that her name was Joyce, and that he was a Monster destined for hell's hottest griddle, she would tell him nothing. Barbara remarked practically that Trevors never gave in to torture, and anyway an unstable canoe was no place to apply thumbscrews. Davis shuddered.

Elinor had been very quiet on the trip. She made herself useful to Joyce, probably too scared of both sides to reach a decision. Davis felt sorry for her.

And then finally they were out of the marsh.

The chief Nicholson told him in her barely intelligible argot that this was a great bay . . . yes, she had heard there was a string of islands closing it off from the mighty waves of the open sea . . . many, many seafolk on many, many islands, all kinds people, Shield Skerry was only a port where coastwise traders dropped off women bound inland, or picked them up; that was all she knew. She wasn't even very curious about the Man.

The rock was a long one, awash at high tide. It was

nearly hidden by the stone walls erected on its back: expert work, massive blocks cut square, a primitive lighthouse where oil fires behind glass burned in front of polished copper reflectors, two long jetties enclosing a small harbor. The canoe buried its nose in a wave, sheeted foam, climbed, rolled, and snuggled down again. Elinor leaned over the side, wished herself dead, and made feeble remarks about the wrath of Father.

Davis looked back. The swamps were a vaporous gray, low in the sea; a storm of shrieking birds made a white wing-cloud under Minos and the two suns, otherwise there were only the great foam-flanked waves that marched out of the west. The water was a chill steely bluish-gray, the wind shrill in his ears.

The surface grew calm between the jetties. Davis saw that a good-sized ship—by Atlantean standards—was in. A counter-weighted wooden crane powered by a capstan wheel was unloading baled cargo, presumably for the upland trade. There was a bustle of strong sun-tanned women, barefoot and clad in wide trousers and halters, their hair cut off just below the ears. Beyond the dock was a small collection of warehouses and dwelling units. They were of stone, with shingle roofs, in the same uncompromising square style as the town wall and the pharos.

The ship was carvel-built, rather broad in the beam, with a high poop and a corroded bronze figurehead—a winged fish. Davis guessed it had a rather deep draught and a centerboard, to maintain freeway in these tricky waters. There was no sign of a mast, but a wooden frame lifted skeletal amidships with a great windmill arrangement turning idly at the peak.

Otherwise the harbor held only a few boats, swift-looking, more or less conventionally yawl-rigged.

"Highest technology I've ever seen here," he remarked.

"What? Oh, you mean their skills," said Barbara. "Yes, they say the seafolk are the best smiths in the world. It's even said a few of their captains can read writing."

"I hope *I* won't have to do that," muttered Valeria behind her veil. "I thought only Doctors knew how."

Davis assumed that the pelagic colonies were old, founded perhaps before the final breakdown of castaway civilization. The sea held abundant food if you knew how

119

to get it. And they must be in closer contact with the Ship than any other tribe. That would doubtless be valuable to them; they would get hints when they sailed past the Holy River estuary and saw the colony of the Doctors.

"What kind of people are they?" he asked.

"We don't know much about them in the uplands," said Barbara. "I've heard they're a violent sort, hard to get along with, even if they do do a lot of trading and ferrying."

And if she thought so . . . !

"Well," said Davis, "we'll find out pretty quick." His stomach was a cold knot within him. "Let me do most of the talking, Val. They won't be so suspicious of my mistakes."

Work at the dock was grinding to a halt. A horn blew brazenly, and women swarmed from the buildings and hurried down tortuous cobbled streets. *"A legate, another legate, and who's that with her?"*

The Nicholson steerswoman brought the canoe expertly to the wharf. The four other swampdwellers laid down their paddles and caught the rope tossed to them. The chief Nicholson bent her head. "We gotcher here, ma'am," she said humbly.

Valeria did not thank her; it wouldn't have been in character. She accepted the hand of a brawny Macklin and stepped up onto the quay. Davis followed. Barbara nudged the wrist-bound Trevor with a knife and urged her after. Elinor slunk behind.

There was a crowd now, pushing and shoving. A few must be police or guards; they wore conical, visored helmets and scaly corselets above their pants. The rest were unarmed. Davis noticed flamboyant tattoos, earrings, thick gold bracelets . . . and on all classes. A Nicholson stood arm in arm with a Latvala; a Craig pushed between a Whitley and a Burke to get a better view; a Holloway carrying a blacksmith's hammer gave amiable blackchat to a Trevor with spear and armor. What . . . ?

Valeria raised her staff. "Quiet!" she shouted.

The babble died away, bit by bit. A gray-haired woman, stocky and ugly, with an official-looking copper brassard on one arm, added a roar: "Shut up, you! It's a legate!"

120

"Yes, ma'am," piped a voice, "but what's that with her?"

The gray woman—an Udall, Davis recognized uneasily—turned to Valeria and bobbed her head. "Begging your pardon, ma'am, we just put in from a rough trip and some of the girls been boozing."

"Are you in charge?" asked Valeria.

"Reckon I am, ma'am, being the skipper of this tub . . . *Fishbird* out o' Farewell Island, she is. Nelly Udall, ma'am, at your service."

Joyce Trevor opened her mouth. She was white with anger. Barbara nudged her and she closed it again.

Valeria stood solemnly for a moment. It grew quiet enough to hear the waves bursting on the breakwater. Then she raised her veiled face and shouted: "Rejoice! The sins of the mothers are washed away and the Men are coming!"

It had the desired effect, though a somewhat explosive one. Davis was afraid his admirers would trample him to death. Nelly Udall stood before him to cuff back the most enthusiastic and bellow at them. "Stand aside! Hold there! Show some respect, you—" What followed brought a maidenly blush to Barbara herself, and she was a cavalry girl.

When the racket had quieted somewhat, Davis decided to take charge. "I am a Man," he said in his deepest voice. "The legate found me in the hills and brought me here. She knows you are a pious people."

"Bless you, dearie," said the Udall through sudden tears. "Sure, we're pious as hell. Any Father-damned thing you want, ma'am, just say so."

"But there is evil afoot," boomed Davis. "I am only the vanguard of the Men. Unless you show yourselves worthy by aiding me to destroy the evil in Atlantis, no others will come."

A certain awe began to penetrate those hard skulls. The show was rolling, and Davis mellowed toward the seafolk.

"I would speak with you and your counselors in private," he said. "I must let you know my will."

Nelly Udall looked confused. "Sure . . . sure, ma'am. Yes, your manship, anything you say. Only—you mean my first mate, maybe?"

121

"Oh . . . no authority here, is there? Well, where does the Udall of the sea-dwellers live?"

"What Udall?" The woman looked around as if expecting one to pop out of some valley. "There's a cousin of mine who's landskipper at Angry Fjord, but that's just a little town."

Davis shook his head. "Who is your ruler—queen, chief, president, whatever you call it? Who makes the decisions?"

"Why, why, Laura Macklin is the preemer, ma'am, if she ain't been voted out," stuttered Nelly. "She's at New Terra, that's the capital. But did you want everybody to come there and vote, ma'am?"

A republic was about the last thing Davis had expected to find. But it was plausible, now that he thought about it. Even on this planet, where the infinite variability of humankind had been unnaturally frozen, it would be hard to establish despotism among a race of sailors. The cheapest catboat with a few disgruntled slaves aboard could sail as fast as the biggest warship.

"I don't get it," said Barbara in a small voice.

"Never mind," said Davis majestically. "I'm afraid you misunderstood me, Captain Udall. Take us to a place where we can talk alone with you."

"Yes, ma'am!" Nelly's eyes came to light on Joyce Trevor's sullen face. She jerked a horny thumb toward the prisoner. "Enemy of yours, ma'am? I'll chop her up personally."

"That will not be required," said Davis. "Bring her along."

Nelly rolled over to Elinor and chucked her under the chip. "Poor dear," she said. "All skin and bones, ain't you? Never mind, chick, we'll fatten you up."

Elinor cringed back and looked at the Udall from terrified eyes.

"Awright, awright, clear a way!" roared Nelly. "Way for the Man! Stand aside there, you! You'll all get a look at him later. Make way!" Her fist emphasized the request, bruisingly, but nobody seemed to mind. Tough lot.

Davis led his party after her, through a narrow street to a smoky kennel with an anchor painted on the gable.

"We'll use this tavern," said Nelly. "Break open a keg of . . . *no,* fishbrains! This is private! We'll roll out a barrel for you when the Man is finished. Git!" She slammed the door in their faces.

Davis coughed. When his eyes were through watering, he saw a room under sooty rafters, filled with benches and tables. A noble collection of casks lined one wall; otherwise, the inn was hung with scrimshaw work and stuffed fish. A whole sealbird roasted in the fireplace.

They parked Joyce in a corner. Elinor crept over beside her. The rest gathered at a table conveniently near one of the barrels while Nelly fetched heroic goblets and tapped the cask.

"Why don't you take off that veil, ma'am?" she asked Valeria. "Even a legate gets thirsty."

"Thanks, I will." The girl did so, grabbed for a beaker, and buried her nose in it. "Whoooo!"

"Oh . . . so sorry, dearie . . . I mean, ma'am. D'you think it was wine? Brandy."

Davis sipped with warned caution. Raw stuff, but it glowed pleasantly inside him. So the sea-dwellers knew about distillation . . . excellent people!

"Now, then, your maleship, say away." Nelly leaned back and sprawled columnar legs across the floor. "Death and corruption! A Man, after all these years!"

Formality was wasted on her, Davis decided. If the sea women didn't go in for it, it wouldn't impress them much. He told her the censored tale he had given at Lysum.

"Heard of those wenches." Nelly snorted. "Well, ma'am . . . sorry, you said it was 'sir,' didn't you? . . . what happened next?"

"This Trevor showed up," said Davis. "She was one of the agents of evil, the same who had whipped Greendale and the other towns into attacking Freetoon. She tried to stir up all Lysum against me. I made her captive, as you see, and we went on down the river till we came here."

"Why didn't you see her gizzard, sir?"

"The Men are merciful," said Davis. "Do you have a place where she can be held incommunicado?"

"A what? We've got a brig."

"That'll do." Davis continued with the rest of his de-

123

mands: passage to the Holy River mouth and an escort to Freetoon, where the lady legate would give the orders of the Ship.

Nelly nodded. "Can do, sir. We don't need to go by way of New Terra, even, if you're in a hurry. There are twenty good crewgirls on the *Fishbird,* and a causeway from the Ship over the swamps . . ."

"We needn't stop at the Ship," said Valeria quickly. "In fact, I'm commanded not to come near it till the Man is on his way back to fetch the rest of the Men. And this has to be kept secret, or we may have more trouble with the, uh, agents of hell."

"Awright, ma'am. We'll just leave the ship at Bow Island and get orspers and ride straight inland. There's a ridge we can follow through the marshes."

Davis frowned. Whatever legate had gone to Freetoon might have planted a story that he really was a Monster, to be killed on sight. Or no, probably not . . . *that* legate had no way of knowing he was the only male human on Atlantis; she'd have to ride back for orders . . .

"The faster the better," he said.

"We'll warp out at Bee-rise tomorrow, sir," said Nelly Udall. She shook her head and stared into her goblet. "A Man! A real live Man! Father, damn it, I'm too old . . . but I've seen you, sir. That's enough for me, I reckon."

CHAPTER XVII

The Shield Skerry brig was a verminous den, but it was solidly built. Davis watched Nelly commute the sentence of its inmates to a few good-natured kicks, toss Joyce within, lock the door, and post a guard to assure that the prisoner saw no one but an attendant who brought meals—and didn't speak even to that person.

Then she led his party down to the dock, where he had supper and delivered a short but telling speech to the assembled women. The inquiries of the preceding legate—whether a Man had been seen—had paved the way for his arrival; there was no one who disbelieved him. He doubted if his injunction to strict secrecy would be respected for many days: it wasn't humanly possible. But the *Fishbird* could head south and be at Holy River in three or four revolutions of Atlantis. Thereafter, given hard riding on relays of orspers, he would be ahead of the news . . . Cosmos! In two Atlantean weeks—a single Earth week—he could be back in space!

Cloud masses piled blackly out of the west, and a smoky-gray overcast hid Ay-set. Wind rose shrill in rigging and streets, surf roared on the breakwater, scud stung his face. He felt the weariness of being hunted. How long had it been already?

"I would retire," he said. "You'll be ready to sail at dawn?"

"Yes, sir, if the girls aren't still too drunk." Nelly gave him a wistful look. "Sure you won't come down to the Anchor with us and . . ."

"Quite sure!" said Barbara and Valeria together.

The crowd trailed them to a long house which Nelly

125

said was reserved for ships' officers. "Best we can do, sir. It's not much but anything we can do for you . . . this way in, sir, my ladies."

There was a sort of common room, with a hall leading off lined by small bedchambers. Elinor slipped into the first; they heard the door bolted behind her. Valeria took the next, then Davis, then Barbara . . . he closed the shutters, turned off the oil lantern, and crept through a sudden heavy darkness into bed. Ahhhh!

Now that he was stretched out and the gale no more than a lullaby, it wasn't easy to fall asleep. Too much to think about, too many memories of home . . .

He was half unconscious when the door opened. As he heard it close again, sleep spilled from him and he sat up. Bare feet groped across the floor.

"Who's that?" Davis fumbled after his dirk, tossed away with the other clothes. His scalp prickled.

"Shhh!" The husky voice was almost in his ear. He reached up and felt a warm roundedness. "Bertie . . . I couldn't stand it any longer, I had to be with you . . ."

Davis made weak fending motions. The girl laughed shyly and slipped under his blankets. He fumbled away, but two strong arms closed about his neck.

"You must know, Bert," she whispered. "You know so much else."

Davis' morality rose in indignation, slipped, and slid. You can only try a man so far. "C'mere!" he said hoarsely.

Her lips closed against his, still inexpert, but she'd learn.

"Bert . . . Bert, darling. I don't know what . . . what this is, to be with a Man . . . but I care for you so much . . ."

"I told you the word was 'love'," he chuckled.

"Did you? When was that?"

"You remember, Val, sweetheart . . . you didn't fool me that night in . . ."

"Val!"

She sat bolt upright and screeched the name into darkness.

"What?" Davis turned cold. "I mean . . . you . . ."

"Val? What's been going on here?"

126

"Oh, no!" groaned Davis. "Barbara, listen, I can explain . . ."

"I'll explain you!" she yelled. A fist whistled past his cheek. It would have been a rough blow if it had connected.

Davis scrambled to get free. The blankets trapped him. Barbara cursed and got her hands on his throat. "Awk!" said Davis. He tore her loose, but she closed in again with ideas of mayhem.

The door opened, and light spilled into the room. The tall red-haired girl carried an axe in her right hand, and the left which held the lantern was scarred.

"What's happening?" barked Valeria.

To the untrained eye, a wrestling match is superficially not unlike certain other sports. Valeria cursed, set down the lantern, and strode forward with lifted axe. Barbara let go, sprang out of bed, snatched up Davis' knife, and confronted her twin.

"So *you've* been fooling around!" she shouted.

"I wouldn't talk if I were you," answered Valeria from clenched jaws. "The minute my back is turned you come oozing in and . . ."

They whirled on Davis. He got out of bed one jump ahead of the axe and backed into a corner. "Now, girls," he stammered. "Ladies, ladies, please!"

Something intimated to him that this was not just the correct approach. The cousins stalked closer.

"Look," begged Davis. "this wasn't my idea, I swear it wasn't, honest!"

Valeria threw her axe to the floor. It stuck there, quivering. "I wouldn't befoul a good weapon with your blood," she said.

Barbara drove his knife into the wall so the blade snapped. "I wouldn't bury him in a fowlcoop," was her contribution.

Their attitude was distinctly more reassuring than it had been, thought Davis. But it still left something to be desired.

"It's all a mistake!" he gibbered.

"The mistake was ever bringing you along," said Valeria. She whirled on Barbara. "And you!"

127

"You moulting corvoid," replied her cousin. "Get out of here before I kill you!"

They neared each other, stiff and claw-fingered. Davis cowered into his corner.

The wind hooted and banged the shutters. Above it, suddenly, he heard a roar. It swept closer, boots racketing on cobblestones, clattering iron, a mob howl.

The Whitleys heard it too. Valeria wrenched her axe from the floor. Barbara darted back to her own room and returned with a bow. The vague light threw their shadows monstrous across the walls.

"What's going on?" said Davis. "What is it . . . ?" He went to open the shutters and look out. A crossbow bolt thudded through the wood. He decided not to open the shutters.

Feet pounded down the hall. Nelly Udall burst into the chamber. There were gashes on her squat body, and the axe in her hand dripped. "Hell and sulfur, Man!" she bawled. "Grab your weapons! They're coming to kill you!"

A Macklin and a youthful Lundgard followed her. They were also wounded, hastily armed, and they were crying.

"What happened?" rattled Davis.

"I bolted the outer door," said Nelly between hoarse breaths. "They'll break it down in a minute." A groan of abused wood chorused her. She turned to Davis, blinking back her own tears. "Are you a Man, dearie, or were you just handing me a line of snakker?"

"I . . . of course I'm a Man," said Davis.

The gray head shook. "Reckon I'll have to take your word for that. I did . . . that's how I got these cuts . . . wreck and plagues! The legate says you aren't. Why didn't you have the sense to kill that shark, child?"

"The legate . . ." Valeria straightened. "I am the legate."

"Yeh? That Trevor says otherwise. And she proved it pretty well."

"*Trevor!*" Davis grabbed the Udall's shoulders and shook her. "What's happened? Is she loose?"

"Yeh," said Nelly in a flat voice. "We was all down at the Anchor, drinking your health, and this Trevor walks in with that Dyckman of yours—says she's the legate and

128

you're a Monster—proved it by running through the rites every mother knows are said at the Ship—challenges your Whitley to do the same . . ." Nelly shook her head again. "It was quite a fight. We three here beat our way out o' the tavern and got here ahead of 'em."

"Elinor!" Barbara's voice seethed.

"She must have sneaked out," said Davis hollowly. "Gone to the brig, told the guard she had new orders from me, set Joyce free . . . what're we going to do now?"

"Fight," answered Nelly. She spat on her hands, waved her axe, and planted herself firmly in the doorway.

There was a final crash, and the mob came down the hall. A Salmon leaped yelling, with drawn knife. Nelly's axe thundered down, the body rolled at her feet. A Hauser jabbed at her with a spear. Barbara shot the Hauser.

It dampened them. The few women who could be seen milled in the narrow corridor. The noise quieted to a tigerish grumble.

Davis took a long breath, summoned all the psychophysiological training they had hammered into him at school, and stepped forward. "Who has been lying about me?" he shouted.

A scarred elderly Damon faced him, bold under the menace of Nelly's axe. "Will you call a truce?" she asked.

"Yes," said Davis. "Hold your fire, Babs. Maybe we can settle this."

Joyce Trevor pushed her way through the crowd. Ragged skirt and matted hair took away none of her frozen dignity. "I say you are a liar and a Monster," she declared.

"Elinor," said Davis, very quietly, still not believing it. "Elinor, why did you do this?"

He glimpsed her near the front of the mob, thin, shaking, and enormous-eyed. Her lips were pale and stiff. "You are," she whispered. "You attacked a legate. The legate says you're a Monster."

Davis smiled wryly. It was too late to be afraid. "I was alone, and there were a lot of Doctors. That's the answer, isn't it? You'll sing a different tune if the Men ever come."

"Shut up, you Monster!" screamed Elinor. "You and those Whitleys kicked me around once too often!"

"I'm not blaming you," said Davis. "It was my fault,

asking you to do what nature never intended you for."

"Someday I'll bash your sludgy brains in, Dyckman," promised Valeria.

Elinor whimpered her way back into the crowd.

"This is a waste of time," snapped Joyce. "If that Whitley is a true legate, let her prove it by reciting the rites."

"Never mind," said Davis. "She isn't."

"You should'a told the truth from the beginning, dearie," said Captain Udall. Her tone reproached him. Paradox: you have to trust people to accomplish your ends, but not all people can be trusted.

"I know . . . now," said Davis. "But it's too late. I *am* a Man. I can bring all the Men here. The legate lies abut me because the Doctors don't want them. It would mean the end of Doctor power."

"I sort of thought that," muttered the Lundgard girl in the room. "That's why I came along."

"Let me to my spaceship," said Davis. "That's all I ask."

"Of course it is," said Joyce. "Women of the sea, once the Monster is aloft how long do you think any of you will live?" She whirled on the crowd. "I lay the eternal curse of Father on anyone who helps this thing!"

Davis cleared his throat and roared back: "Father is another lie! If he exists, let him strike me dead! If he doesn't, you can see for yourselves how the Doctors have lied!"

"*We* are Father's instruments," shouted Joyce. "Kill it!"

Nelly hefted her axe, grinning. "Who's next?" she inquired.

"The Men are coming," said Davis smoothly. "Whatever happens to me, the Men will come in another generation. And they'll punish or reward according to how the first Man on Atlantis was treated."

That was a forty-carat whopper. The Service never took revenge on a society, or on any member thereof who acted in terms of its structure. But Davis was in no mood to explain Union law.

He heard feet shuffle in the corridor, voices buzz and break, spears drag on the floor. And there was the sound

130

of new arrivals, a few pro-Davis women stamping in and one pronouncing the lovely, eloquent, rational words: "Whoever touches the Man gets hung!"

The bulk of Shield Skerry didn't know what to think; they inclined to believe the legate, but they had cooled off just a little. Women have slightly less tendency to act in mobs than men do. Davis straightened, licked his lips, and walked forward.

"I'm going out," he said. "Make way."

Barbara, Valeria, Nelly and her two companions, followed at his heels. A handful of determined roughnecks shoved through the paralyzed crowd, toward him, to join him.

"Kill them!" yelled Joyce. "Kill them or Father curse you!"

Barbara whirled around, her crossbow raised. "If you try anything," she said bleakly, "the legate dies first."

Davis brushed past Elinor. She hid her eyes from him. He felt no anger; it was useless. What he had to do now was clear out before somebody got heated up enough to break this explosive quiet.

As gently as possible, he went through the packed hall and the jammed common room. There were a score of armed women with him now, to form a comforting circle. They started for the quay.

The wind raved in coalsack streets. Davis shuddered and forced himself to forget the cold and the heavy waves beating beyond the harbor. He heard the crowd follow, but it was too dark for him to see them.

Barbara—he felt the hard stock of her arbalest— whispered venomously: "Don't think I'm coming along for your sake, you slimy double-face. I haven't any choice."

Davis stumbled on a cobblestone and swore. The wind whipped his oath from him. These few dozen meters were the longest walk he had ever taken.

When they emerged from canyon-like walls, onto the wharf, enough light to see by trickled down from the pharos. Nelly led the way toward her ship. "I'm staking one hell of a lot on your really being a Man," she cried into the wind.

"Thanks," said Davis inadequately.

"I don't dare believe anything else," she said in an empty voice.

A gangplank was thrown from quay to hull. Davis could just make out the crowd, where it swirled in the shadows. It would be no trick for them to shoot at him. But praise all kindly fates, they were used to thinking for themselves in a rough tarry-thumbed fashion; they were still chewing on the unknown.

Joyce would talk them around soon enough, but by then he would be gone.

Valeria edged close to him and hissed: "Yes, I'll believe you're a Man too . . . and the hell with all Men! I'm only coming because I haven't any other choice."

Nelly tramped over the gangplank. When she had a deck beneath her feet, she seemed to draw strength from it. "All aboard, you scuts! Man the capstan! Look lively or I'll beat your ears off!"

She went aft, up on the poop to a nighted helm. The other women scurried about, doing incomprehensible things with ropes and pulleys. The great windmill, sweeping within a meter of the main deck, jerked, whined, and resumed more slowly. There was a white threshing at the stern, and the *Firebird* moved out of the harbor.

CHAPTER XVIII

Morning was gray over an ice-gray sea, where waves snorted from horizon to horizon. A dim streak in the east was land. The ship wallowed and yawed.

Davis emerged from one of the little cabins under the poop to find the fo'c'sle drawn up before a small galley for breakfast. He joined the line, hugging a cloak he had found, close to his skin. Valeria was ahead of him, Barbara already eating in the lee of the bulwarks. Both ignored him. The sailors—mostly young women of the more warlike families, he noticed—chattered happily, but he was in no mood for their conversation.

His eyes went over the decks. Aft was the wheelhouse and a sort of binnacle—yes, they undoubtedly had some kind of compass. The main deck held the galley and the cargo hatches. Up by the prow, immediately behind the figurehead, was a harpoon-gun catapult.

The windmill faced into the stiff northwesterly wind. It squealed less than he would have expected—must be well oiled. From the gear housing at the peak an ironbound shaft went down through the derrick, into the hold, turning.

Neat arrangement, thought Davis. There must be a set of universal gears at the windmill head, so it could swing directly into any breeze. Its rotation was transmitted by shafts and other gears to a screw propeller. The *Fishbird* could sail straight against the wind if the skipper chose. Of course, the gears would have to be ground with précision, and being of rather soft steel would need frequent replacement; but if you didn't know how to build a steam engine, it was a good idea.

Nelly Udall waddled down from the poop as he got his

tray. " 'Morning, dearie," she boomed. "Sea bother you?"

"No," said Davis. A spaceman, trained to all gravities from zero on up, didn't mind a little rolling.

"Good. Kind of hard to believe in a seasick Man, eh? Haw, haw, haw!" Nelly slapped his back so he staggered. "I like you, chick, damn if I don't."

"Thanks," said Davis weakly.

"Come into my cabin. We'd better talk this over."

It was a very small room. They sat on her bunk and Davis said: "I'm not sure what to do next. Go on to Holy River?"

"Wouldn't recommend it," said Nelly. She took out a pipe and began stuffing it with greenish flakes from a jar. Davis' eyes lit up. It wasn't tobacco, but it could be smoked. Her words brought him up cold. "Not unless you want a dart in your liver."

"Huh?"

"Think a bit, dearie. That Father-damned legate has preached hellfire to 'em back at Shield. By now, the boats must be headed for the Ship to bring the glad tidings. They can sail rings around one of these propeller buckets, if the wind is right . . . and it is, for tacking, anyway. Time we get to Bow Island, all that country will be up in arms."

"Glutch!" strangled Davis.

Nelly ignited a punk stick with her fire piston, got the pipe going, and blew nauseous clouds. "Sure you aren't seasick, duck?" she asked. "All of a sudden you don't look so good."

"What're we going to *do?*" mumbled Davis.

"Right now," Nelly told him, "I'm bound for my home port, Farewell. Got friends there, and nobody'll think to bring them the news for a while. Won't be nobody to conterdick whatever you want to say. And what'll that be?"

She watched him with expectant little eyes. Davis stared through the rippled glass of the port. A wave smacked against it, water streamed down and the ship lurched.

"Think they'll still support us when they do hear?"

"I know a lot who will, dearie. I did, didn't I? Eighteen of us, besides your two Whitleys, and *that* was with the legate hooting in our faces. We've gotten almighty sick of the Doctors, I can tell you. We see more of 'em than the uplanders do, the . . ." Nelly devoted a few minutes to a

134

rich catalogue of the greed, arrogance, and general snottiness of the Doctors.

They couldn't be quite such villains. Very likely, a number of them honestly thought he must be a Monster; his advent hadn't fitted in with the elaborate eschatology they seemed to have evolved. Others were doubtless more cynical about it, but Davis could not regard that as a crime.

However—he knew enough Union law to be sure that just about anything he did to the Doctors would be all right with the Coordination Service. This was not a matter of passing anthropomorphic judgments on some non-human civilization; Homo sapiens values were rigorously established, and they included a normal family life.

The idea grew slowly. He scarcely heard the Udall rumble on: "I reckon we can raise a few shiploads. We can go far up the coast, then strike inland to get at your boat from the rear . . ."

"No!" said Davis.

"Hm?"

"Too risky. It'll be guarded as heavily as they can manage. The Doctors aren't going to give up till they've seen my pickled head. And they may have tools enough left in the Ship to take to Freetoon and demolish my boat. We've got to act fast."

"So . . ." Nelly waited, her pipe smoldering in stumpy fingers.

"So we get a fleet together at Farewell . . . yes. If you really believe your girls are ready to hazard their lives to be free— Do you?"

Nelly smiled. "Chick, with that beard and that voice you can talk 'em into storming hell gate."

"It won't be quite that bad," said Davis. "I hope. What we're going to do is storm the Ship."

CHAPTER XIX

High tide on battle day was just after Bee-rise. As the morning fog broke up into ragged gray streamers, the rebel fleet lay to at Ship city.

Davis stood on the *Fishbird*'s deck and watched his forces move in. There were twenty other propeller craft, and about as many fishing schooners and smaller boats. Their windmills and white sails were like gull wings across waters muddy-blue, rippled and streaked by an early breeze. At their sterns flew the new flag he had designed. His girls were quite in love with the Jolly Roger.

The rebels numbered some two thousand women from the Farewell archipelago. It had been estimated that there were half again as many at the Ship—but less tough, less experienced in fighting (the seafolk were not above occasional piracy), a number of them children or aged. The odds didn't look so bad.

Valeria stamped her feet so the deck thudded. "I'm going ashore," she said mutinously.

"No, you don't, chickabiddy." Nelly Udall twirled a belaying pin. "Got to keep some guard over the Man. What's the use of it all if he gets himself skewered?"

Barbara nodded coldly. "She's right, as anybody but a gruntbrain like you could see," she added. "Not that I wouldn't rather guard a muckbird! But if our friends are stupid enough to *want* the Men, I'll play along."

Davis sighed. In the three Atlantean weeks since they left Shield Skerry, neither of the cousins had spoken to him, or to each other without a curse. After the hundredth rebuff, he had given up trying to reconcile them.

Yet somehow he couldn't just say to Evil with them and console himself elsewhere. He remembered strolling alone on the cliffs of Farewell one day. It was chill and cloudy,

136

the surf ramped below him, and wind flung scud far up into his face and hissed in harsh grass. Suddenly a girl appeared from a thicket. She was a Lundgard, young and pretty. More than the weather had flushed her face and brightened her eyes. As she approached him, he saw with unease that she wore under her cloak only the briefest of tunics.

"Hail to ye," she said.

"Uh, hello," he faltered.

She stood hands on hips, looking him up and down. At last she smiled. "It'll be more fun than awesome, I think," she said.

"What will?" he gaped.

She took off her cloak and spread it on the ground. Three deft motions dropped the tunic beside it. She opened her arms wide. Her blush crept astonishingly far downward, but her tone was calm. "If you're in truth the Man, here I am for your use."

"Ulp!" said Davis. He backed away. "But, but, but—"

"Please," she begged. "I made a bet you would."

"Oh, no!" groaned Davis.

It seemed most ungentlemanly to cost her her wager. But that morning he had spied Barbara and Valeria on the street. He had called to them, and they turned their faces away. It was the reason he had come on this walk. He wished he could rid himself of the ridiculous obsession that made all other women nearly meaningless. But it wasn't possible.

"I'm sorry." He hurried on past the girl.

She looked after him a moment, smiled wryly and picked up her clothes again. "Well," she said, "win one, lose one."

Davis was positively glad that now all such chances were behind him. He had hated himself for wasting them.

Nelly picked up a megaphone and bawled at a vessel maneuvering toward the wharf. "Sheer off! Sheer off or you'll pile up!"

The Ship must have been badly crippled, thought Davis, to land here; probably it had come down where it could, on the last gasp of broken engines. The walls which now enclosed it had been built on a hill that just barely stuck out over high tide. Eastward lay the marshes, a dreary

137

land where a broad stone causeway slashed through toward the distance-blued peaks of the Ridge.

There must have been heavy earth-moving equipment and construction robots in the Ship's cargo. A few thousand women could not have raised this place by hand. Now the machines were long ago worn out, but their work remained.

The city was ringed by white concrete walls five meters high, with a square watchtower at each corner. The walls fell straight into the water of high tide or the mud of ebb: inaccessible save by the causeway entering the eastern gate or the wide quay built out from the west side. Against this dock the nearest rebel boats were lying to. Gangplanks shot forth and armored women stormed onto the wharf. The ships beyond nudged the inner ones, forming a bridge for the rest of the crews. The *Fishbird* lay just outside the little fleet.

Davis let his eyes wander back to the city. He could see the tops of buildings above the walls, the dome-roofed Carolinian architecture of three centuries ago. And he could see the great whaleback of the Ship itself, three hundred meters long from north wall to south wall, metal still bright but a buckled spot at the waist to show how hard it had landed.

Barbara looked at the yelling seafolk. She was clad like them: visored helmet on her ruddy hair, tunic of steely scaled orcfish hide, trousers, spike-toed boots. The accessories included axe, knife, crossbow and quiver—she had become a walking meat grinder. She and Valeria still kept their lassos around their shoulders.

Davis, equipped like them, felt the same sense of uselessness. Not that he *wanted* to face edged metal; but when women were ready to die for his sake . . .

Bee struck long rays into his eyes. Ay was so close as to be hidden by the glare of the nearer sun. Monos brooded overhead in the gigantic last quarter. There was a storm on the king planet, he could almost see how the bands and blotches writhed.

Horns blew on the walls, under the Red Cross flag of the city. Women, lithe tough legates and acolytes, were appearing in cuirass, greaves, and masking helmet, all of burnished metal. Crossbows began to shoot.

138

There was no attempt to batter down the double door at the end of the quay; it was of solid iron, the hinges buried in concrete. A howling mass of sailors raised ladders and swarmed skyward.

"Cosmos!" murmured Davis.

A Doctor shoved at one of the ladders, but there was a good nautical grapnel on its end; it could not easily be thrown. Davis saw her unlimber a long rapier. The first rebel up got it through the throat and tumbled knocking off the woman below her.

"Let me go!" yelled Valeria.

"Hold still," rapped Nelly. Her worried eyes went to Davis. "I didn't think they'd have so good a defense, chick. They've never had to fight, but it seems they were always prepared. We'd better get them licked fast."

He nodded. They had only a couple of hours before the tide dropped so far that any ship which remained would be stranded till the next high. There were locks to take care of ordinary visitors, but a vessel in such a basin would be trapped as effectively as one sitting in the mud.

"So we stay," growled Barbara. "Isn't that the idea?"

"Yeh," said Davis. He drew hard on a borrowed pipe. "Only the Doctors must have raised a local army from the upland towns, to keep us from getting to Freetoon. Now they'll send for its help. If things go badly, I'd like a way to retreat."

"*You* would," she agreed, and turned her back on him.

Axes, spears, swords clashed up on the wall, bolts and darts gleamed in the cool early light. The Doctor fighters were rapidly being outnumbered. One of them, in a red cloak of leadership, winded a horn. Her women fought their way toward her.

Nelly Udall jumped up and down, cackling. "We win!" she cried, and pounded Davis on the back. "We've got the walls already!"

He staggered, caught the rail. It couldn't be that simple! No, the Doctor forces had rallied and were streaming down a stairway into their town. A slim young Burke cried triumph; he could hear the hawk-shriek above all the racket and see how her dark hair flew as she planted the Jolly Roger on the city wall.

The women on the dock poured antlike up the ladders.

It grew thick with rebels above the Ship.

Something moved between the crenels of the two flanking towers. Big wooden flywheels spun on the parapets. Davis could see Doctors manning an intricate machine. A ratcheted belt fed to grooves in each wheel, a rain of darts gushed out.

Primitive machine gun, he thought wildly. *But it works!*

Slaughter raged along the wall. The young Burke who carried the flag dropped it, clawed at her breast, and toppled off. A Tottino fell, dripping blood on the concrete.

"Get this damned bilgebucket in!" howled Valeria. She fired wildly at the nearest tower, tears whipping down her face.

"No," groaned Nelly. "The Man . . ."

Barbara lifted her axe. "Hell rot the Man! They're being butchered up there! Land us!"

A party of sea women reached the stairway and started down into the city. The Doctors defended it with sword and spear and bow; it was too narrow a passage to force in a minute. Murder glittered and whistled from the parapets.

Someone cried out, picked up the fallen flag, and raced for a tower. A hundred girls streamed after her. They couldn't all be cut down. They got into the cone of safety, below which the machine could not be depressed, and shook their spears at the wall before them.

Nelly roared into her megaphone: "Another ladder! Another ladder, two others, you witless ninny-hammers!"

A troop of older women, held in reserve, ran ashore with the ladders. They planted them against the city walls, next to the towers. The rebels above dragged them up and laid them against the battlements.

Up and over! There was a red flash of axes. The dart throwers whirred on, spewing no more . . . until somebody grabbed one, pulled down the feeding lever, and raked the stairway.

Nelly grabbed Davis and whirled him a wild stomp around the deck. "We got 'em, we got 'em, we got 'em!" she caroled. Planks shuddered beneath her.

The storming party went down the stairs. Others followed, an armored wave up the ladders and into the city. The Red Cross was pulled down from its tower and the Jolly Roger flapped in its place, skull grinning over a hundred corpses and two hundred wounded.

Davis felt sick. His whole culture was conditioned against war; it remembered too well how cities had gone up in radioactive smoke and barrenness crept stealthily over green hills.

"Scared?" jeered Barbara. "You're safe enough."

"Sure," said Valeria. "If it looks like you might get hurt after all, we'll take you away."

"I'm not going to retreat!" said Davis in a raw voice.

"Yes, you will, duck, if we got to," said Nelly. "If you get killed, what's for us?" Her seamed face turned grimly inland. "We've got to win . . . no choice . . . if the Doctors win, there'll never be another baby on the islands."

That was what drove them, thought Davis. And an even deeper need, which made political grudges the merest excuse given to the conscious mind. Instinct said that a machine was too unsafe a way of bringing new life into the universe.

Except for the casualties and a few guards, nearly the whole rebel force was now out of sight within the city. He could just hear the noise of battle. It seemed to be receding . . . that meant his side was driving the Doctors back.

So what if he won? A victory where you yourself did nothing was no victory for a man.

Damn! His pipe had gone out.

The iron doors were flung open. He could not see through them from where the *Fishbird* lay, but it showed that the west end of town was firmly held by his side.

"I think we'll have the place before ebb," said Nelly. "But then what do we do?"

"We'll have the parthenogenetic apparatus," Davis reminded her. "Not to mention the prestige of victory. We'll own the planet."

"Oh . . . yeah, that's right. Keep forgetting. I'm growing old, dearie." Nelly waved her axe. "But I'd still like to part the hair on a few Doctors!"

There was a shriek through the doorway.

Sailors poured out of it, falling over each other, hurling their weapons from them in blind panic. A couple of hundred women made for the ships.

"What's happened?" bawled Nelly. "Avast, you hooti-nannies! Stop that!" She went into a weeping tirade of pro-fanity.

Barbara snatched the megaphone from her. "Pull in!" she cried. "We're going ashore!"

The helmswoman looked ill, but yanked a signal cord. Down in the hold, the engineers shoved levers to engage the windmill. It caught with a metal howl and the *Fishbird* swung around. The forward watch went to the capstan, the anchor rose and the ship wallowed across a narrow stretch of open water.

Nelly Udall waited mutely. Her vessel bumped against one of the docked schooners. Two girls at the bulwarks flung out grapples.

"Let's go," snapped Valeria. She leaped onto the schooner deck, axe aloft.

Barbara saw Davis follow. "No!" she yelled.

"Yes," he answered harshly. "I've stood enough."

She grabbed his arm. He shook her off, blind with fury, and dashed across to the wharf.

The mob was still coming out of the door and over the quay to mill around on the ships. One anchor was already weighed. Davis grabbed a Craig and whirled her around.

"What's the matter?" he shouted.

She gave him an unseeing look. "The fire," she whim-pered. "Oh, the fire!"

He slapped her. "Talk sense! What happened in there?"

"We . . . street fighting . . . Doctor troop . . . flame, white flame and it *burned* our forward line . . ." The Craig collapsed.

Davis felt something sink within him. He turned slowly to the *Fishbird* crew. "Did you ever hear of a fire weapon?" he asked.

"No," said Nelly. "No, never."

"It's Father himself!" gasped a Macklin.

"Shut up!" rapped Davis. "I know what it is. They must have found my blaster up by Freetoon and the legate took it back here. Maybe records in the Ship describe blasters." He shook his head numbly. "Chilluns, this is not a good thing."

"What are we going to do?" whispered Barbara.

142

"We're going to get that blaster," he sa.
weapon. There's nothing supernatural abou.
stream. And there's only one of them."

"You'll be killed," said Valeria. "No, wait here, ⊾
. . ."

"Follow me," he said. "If you dare!"

They trotted after him, a dozen from the *Fishbird* and as many more from the retreat whose morale had picked up.

He went through the doorway and saw an ordered gridiron of paved streets between tall concrete houses. The Ship rose huge at the end of all avenues. This close, he could even read the name etched on the bows, *New Hope*. It seemed a cruel sort of name.

From two other streets came the noise of fighting. The battle had spread out, and most of its groups had not yet seen the fire gun. They would, though, if he didn't hurry; and that would be the end of all rebellion.

"We went down this way," pointed a Latvala from the original party. "Three streets down, and then we met this band of enemies at our left."

Davis jogged between closed doors and broad glass windows. Looking in, he saw that the Doctors did themselves well; no such luxury existed elsewhere on Atlantis. He could understand their reluctance to abandon such a way of life.

He skidded to a halt. The Doctors were coming around the corner ahead of him.

There were about twenty. A party of young legates, their helmets facelessly blank, spread from wall to wall with interlocked shields. Behind them lifted swords and halberds.

"Get them!" shouted Nelly.

Three girls sprang ahead of Davis. One of them was a Whitley; he thought for a moment she was one of *his* Whitleys and then saw Barbara and Valeria still flanking him.

Over the shield tops lifted a Burke face. It was an old face, toothless and wrinkled under a tall bejeweled crown, and the body was stooped beneath white robes. But his blaster gleamed in a skinny hand.

143

Davis flung out his arms and dove to the ground, carrying Barbara and Valeria with him. Blue-white fire sizzled overhead.

The three young girls fell, blasted through. It could have been Val or Barbara lying there, thought Davis wildly. He remembered how he loved them.

He rolled over, into a doorway. "Get out!" he screamed.

His gang were already stampeded. Nelly stood firm, and Barbara and Valeria were beside him. Nelly threw her axe; it glanced off a shield, and the legate stumbled against the old Doctor. Her next shot missed, and Nelly pumped thick legs across the street.

She hit the door with one massive shoulder. It went down in splinters. Davis sprang into a sybarite's parlor.

"Quick!" he said. "Out the back way!"

Two legates appeared in the doorframe. Barbara's crossbow snapped twice. Valeria and Nelly were already out of the parlor.

Davis followed and saw a stair. "Give me your lasso, Babs," he said. "I have an idea."

"We're all coming." She uncoiled the rope as they pounded after him.

A bedroom overlooked the street. Davis shoved up the window. The blaster party was just underneath. He threw his axe down, missed the old witch, and cursed. Her gun swiveled toward him.

Barbara shoved him aside, leaned out the window, and sent her lariat soaring. It closed around the chief Doctor; Barbara grinned and drew the noose taut.

"Help!" screamed the Burke. "I've been roped!"

Davis sprang into the street. Almost, he skewered himself on one of the halberds. He landed on an armored legate and both went down with a rattle and a gong.

She didn't move. Davis jumped up and landed a left hook to the nearest jaw. Valeria's lasso snaked from the window, fastened to something. She came sliding down it with her axe busy. Nelly followed. Barbara took a few judicious shots before joining them.

The old one snarled. She fought free and reached for the blaster. "Oh, no, you don't!" Davis put his foot on it. A rapier struck his scaly coat and bent upward, raking his

144

cheek. He kicked, and the woman reeled off to trip somebody else. A slender form closed with him; a dagger felt for his throat. He got his hands on the waist, lifted her up, and tossed her into the melee.

Nelly had picked up an axe. "Whoopee!" she bellowed, and started chopping. Barbara and Valeria stood back to back, their weapons a blur in front of them. Davis was still too inhibited to use whetted steel on women, but every blow he dealt shocked loose some of his guiltiness.

The fight was over in a few minutes. Davis stooped for the blaster and spent another minute incinerating the Doctors' dropped weapons. "Let's go," he panted.

"Are you just going to leave these scuts here?" Nelly pointed at the enemy casualties.

"Sure. We've pulled their teeth." Davis stuck the gun in his belt. "Can't you get it through your thick head, this fight is for everybody on Atlantis—Doctors included?"

"No," she grunted. "Oh, well."

They went on down the street. There was a narrow passage between the Ship's ruined gravity cones and the wall. On the other side lay a broad square, lined with impressive temples, a few dead and wounded women strewn across it.

But no more sound of fighting . . . odd!

A sailor troop emerged from behind one of the columned sanctuaries. "It's the Man!" squealed somebody. They ran toward him and drew up, flushed. The leader gave a sketchy salute.

"I think we just about have the town, sir," she puffed. "I was patrolling on the east end. Didn't see anyone."

"Good!" Davis shuddered his relief. He *could* not have used a blaster on women; the memory of the dead Whitley girl was burned too deeply in him.

"Get our people together here," he said. "Mount guards on the towers and at the gates. Round up all the Doctors left, herd 'em into one of these chapels . . . .and don't use them for target practice! Set up a sickbay for the wounded—and that means enemy wounded, too. Nelly, you take charge. I want a look around."

He walked through empty streets. Behind him he could hear cheers and trumpets, the tramp of feet and triumphal clang of arms, but he was in no mood for it.

145

Minos was a thin sliver, with Bee sliding close. Nearly eclipse time . . . had all this really taken three hours? It seemed like a nightmare century.

The Whitleys trailed him. He heard one of them speak: "I take a lot back, Val. You fought pretty good."

"Hell, Babs, you're no slouch yourself. After all, darling, you are identical with me."

The street opened on another plaza, a narrow one that ran the length of the east wall. There was a doorway in the middle, with wrought-iron gates. Davis looked through the bars to the causeway and the marshes. Mud gleamed on the ridge which the road followed, birds screamed down after flopping fish. The tide was ebbing, the ships stranded . . . but what the Evil, they had won, hadn't they?

Hold on there!

The highway bent around a clump of saltwater trees three kilometers from the city. Davis saw what approached from the other side and grabbed the bars with both hands.

"An army!" he croaked.

Rank after rank poured into view. He thought he could hear the slap of orsper feet and the war-cries lifted among haughty banners. Now he saw leather corselets, iron morions, boots and spurs and streaming cloaks. They were the hill people and they were riding to the relief of the Doctors.

"A couple of thousand, at least," muttered Barbara. "The legates must have gone after them as soon as we attacked . . . They've been waiting around to kill you, my dearest . . ." She whirled on him, her visored face pressed against his side. "And it's too late to retreat—we're boxed in!"

"Not too late to fight!" Valeria dashed toward the inner town, shouting. Sea women on the walls lifted horns to lips and wailed an alarm.

Davis looked at the gate. It was locked, but it could be broken apart. His hand went to the blaster. Before Cosmos! That would stop them—it was the least he could do for these girls who trusted him.

No!

The rebel army pelted into the plaza. Right and left, arbalesters swarmed up the staircases to the walls. The dart

146

throwers swiveled about on their turrets. *Cosmos,* thought Davis, *hasn't there been enough killing?*

Behind him, Nelly Udall scurried along the ranks of the women, pushing them into a semblance of order. Davis regarded them. Tired faces, hurt faces, lips that tried to be firm and failed; they would fight bravely, but they hadn't a chance against fresh troops.

The pirate flag fluttered defiantly up on a staff over the gate. The nearing cavalry whooped. Bolts whistled to make a rag of it.

"Shoot!" screamed Barbara. "Burn them down, Bert!"

The blaster was in his hand. He looked at it, dazedly.

Up on the parapets, the dart throwers began to clatter. Orspers reared, squawked, went off the road into the mud and flapped atrophied wings. The charge came to a clanging halt, broke up, fought its way back along the road . . . it stopped. Leaders trotted between panicked riders, haranguing them.

Hill women dismounted. Their axes bit at a roadside tree. It wouldn't take them long to make a battering ram. They would slog forward under the dart fire; they would be slaughtered and others would take their place. The ram would get into the cone of safety and the gates come down.

"When they're in range," leered Nelly, "let 'em have it!"

Bee slipped behind Minos. The planet became a circle of blackness ringed with red flame. Of all the moons, only firefly Aegeus was visible. Stars glittered coldly forth. A wind sighed across the draining marshes, dusk lay heavy on the world.

"Let me try something," said Davis.

He fired into the air. Livid lightning burned across heaven, a small thunder cracked in its wake. Screams came from the shadow army on the road; he fired again and waited for them to flee.

"Hold fast! Stay where you are, Father damn you!" The voices drifted hoarse through the gloom. "If we let the Monster keep the Ship, you'll die with never another child in your arms!"

Davis shook his head. He might have known it.

Someone clattered up the road. Four short trumpet

147

blasts sent the sea birds mewing into the sudden night. "Truce call," muttered Valeria. "Let 'em come talk. Answer the signal."

"Might as well," said Nelly. "I don't *want* to see 'em fried alive." She took a horn from the girl beside her and winded it.

The mounted woman approached. She was an Udall herself. Barbara squinted through the murk at the painted insignia. "Bess of Greendale!" she hissed. "Kill her!"

Davis could only think that the Doctors' desperation had been measured by their sending clear up to Greendale for help. The swamp and the upper valley must be aswarm with armies intent on keeping him from his boat.

"No," he said. "It's a parley, remember?"

The Udall rode scornfully up under the walls. "Is the Monster here?"

"The Man is here," said Barbara.

Davis stepped into view, peering through iron bars and thick twilight. "What do you want?"

"Your head, and the Ship back before you ruin the life machine."

"I can kill you," said Davis. "I can kill your whole army. Watch!" He blasted at the road. Stone bubbled and ran molten.

Bess Udall fought her plunging orsper to a halt. "Do you think that matters?" she panted. "We're fighting for every unborn kid on Atlantis. Without the machine we might as well die."

"But I'm not going to harm the damned machine!"

"So *you* say. You've struck down the Doctors. I wouldn't trust you dead without a stake through your heart."

"Oh, hell," snarled Valeria. "Why bother? Let 'em come and find out you mean business."

Davis stared at the blaster. "No—there are decent limits."

He shook himself and looked out at the vague form of the woman. "I'll make terms," he said.

"What?" yelled Barbara and Valeria together.

"Shut up. Bess, here's my offer. You can enter the town. The sea people will return to their ships and sail away at next high tide. In return, they'll have access to the life machine just as they always did."

"And you?" grated the Udall. "We won't stop fighting till you're dead."

"I'll come out," said Davis. "Agreed?"

"No!" Barbara leaped at him. He swung his arm and knocked her to the ground.

"Stand back!" His voice rattled. "I'm a Man."

Bess Udall stared at him. "Agreed," she said. "Open the gates and come out. I swear to your terms by Father."

The rebels shuffled forward, shadow mass in a shadow world. Davis could barely make out his Whitleys. Valeria was helping Barbara up.

"Don't move," he said. "It isn't worth it . . . my life . . . The Men will be here in another generation anyway."

His blaster boomed, eating through the lock on the gates. He pushed them open, the hot iron burning his hands, and trod through. With a convulsive gesture, he tossed the blaster into a mudpool.

"All right," he said. "Let's go."

Bess edged her orsper close to him. "Move!" she barked. A few women surged from the gateway. She brandished her spear. "Stand back, or the Monster gets this right now!"

Minos was a ring of hellfire in the sky.

"Wait!"

It was a Whitley voice. Davis turned. He felt only an infinite weariness; let them kill him and be done with it.

He couldn't see whether it was Barbara or Valeria who spoke: "Hold on there! It's us who make the terms."

"Yes?" growled the rider. Her spear poised over Davis.

"We have the life machine. Turn him back to us or we'll smash it and kill every Doctor in town before you can stop us!"

A sighing went through the rebels. Nelly cursed them into stillness. "That's right, dearie," she cried. "What the blazes is a bloody machine worth when we could have the Men?"

Davis waited, frozenly.

The Whitley walked closer, cat-gaited. "These are *our* terms," she said flatly. "Lay down your arms. We won't hurt you. By Father, I never knew what it means to be a Man till now! You can keep the town and the ma-

149

chine—yes, the Doctors—if you want. Just let us bring the Man to his ship and bring the Men back for us!"

Bess Udall's spear dropped to the ground.

"You don't know he's a Man," she stammered.

"I sure do, sister. Do you think we'd have stormed the Holy Ship for a Monster?"

Night and silence lay thick across the land. A salt wind whined around red-stained battlements.

"Almighty Father," choked Bess. "I think you're right."

She whirled her orsper about and dashed down the road.

Davis stood there, hoping he wouldn't collapse.

He heard them talking in the orsper host. It seemed to come from very far away. His knees were stiff as he walked slowly back toward the gate.

Several riders hurried after him. They pulled up and jumped to the ground and laid their weapons at his feet.

"Welcome," said a voice. "Welcome, Man."

The sun swung from behind Minos and day burned across watery wastes and the far eastern mountains.

Davis let them cheer around him. Barbara knelt at his feet, hugging his knees. Valeria pushed her way close to lay her lips on his. "Bert," she whispered. He tasted tears on her mouth. "Bert, darling."

"Take either of us," sobbed Barbara. "Take us both if you want."

"Well, hooray for the Man!" said Nelly. "Three chee —whoops! Catch him! I think he's fainted!"

CHAPTER XX

It had been a slow trip through the valley. They had to stop and be feasted at every town along the way.

Davis Bertram stood in tall grass, under a morning wind, and looked up the beloved length of his spaceship. He whistled, and the airlock opened and the ladder descended for him.

"I'll be back," he said clumsily. "It'll take me a little longer to reach Nerthus—I want to be sure I don't hit that vortex—but inside a hundred of your days the Men will be here."

And what would they say when he walked into Stellamont wearing this garb of kilt, feather cloak, and war-bonnet? He grinned at the idea.

The Freetoon army was drawn up in dress parade a few meters off. Sunlight flamed on polished metal and oiled leather, plumes nodded and cloaks fluttered in the breeze. More of their warriors had survived the invasion than he expected. They came out of the woods to worship him as their deliverer when he ordered the town set free. A cheap enough deed; local sovereignty would soon be obsolete here.

Gaping civilians trampled the meadows behind them. Davis wondered how many of their babies he had touched, for good luck. Well, it beat kissing the little apes . . . not that it wouldn't be nice to have a few of his own someday.

Barbara and Valeria stood before him. Under the burnished helmets their faces were drawn tight, waiting for his word.

His cheeks felt hot. He looked away from their steady green eyes and dug at the ground with his sandals.

"You're in charge here," he mumbled. "If you really want to make Freetoon a republic . . . and it'd be a big help—you folk have a difficult period of adjustment ahead . . . at least one of you has to stay and see the job is done right."

"I know," said Valeria. Her tone grew wistful. "You'll bring that psych machine you spoke of to . . . make her forget you?"

"Not forget," said Davis. "Only to feel differently about it. I'll do better than that, though. I'll bring a hundred young men, and you can take your pick!"

"All right," said Valeria. "I pick you."

"Hoy, there!" said Barbara.

Davis wiped sweat off his brow. What was a chap to do, anyway? He felt trapped.

"It'd be better if you both stayed," he stuttered. "You'll have a . . . a rough time . . . fitting into civilization."

"Do you really want that?" asked Barbara coolly.

"No," said Davis. "Good Cosmos, no!"

After all, he was a survey man. He wouldn't be close to civilization for very long at a time, ever. Even a barbarian woman, given spirit and intelligence, could be trained into a spacehand.

And a few gaucheries wouldn't matter. A Whitley in formal dress would be too stunning.

"Well, then," said Valeria. Her knuckles tightened around her spearshaft. "Take you choice."

"I can't," said Davis. "I just can't."

The cousins looked at each other. They nodded. One of them took a pair of dice from her pouch.

"One roll," said Barbara.

"High girl gets him," said Valeria.

Davis Bertram stood aside and waited. He had the grace to blush.

AUTHOR'S NOTE

Science fiction readers are interested in science, and it's a pity they get so little of it. With a few honorable exceptions, writers are all too prone to create either rank impossibilities or minor variations on the Earth and the Western civilization we already know. So far, to my knowledge, only Hal Clement has actually set forth his calculations, and his *"Mission of Gravity"* is therefore a fascinating logical exercise. The present story makes no claim to such intellectual stature, but a few background details which could not get into the narrative may be of interest.

A fantastic yarn is properly allowed only one assumption contrary to fact. In the present case, I have made the postulate—which may be true, for all anyone knows—. that relativity gives only a partial picture of the structure of the universe, and that someday new discoveries will be made which will force us to modify our physical theory.

I assume, in short, that faster-than-light travel is possible. This is not supposed to be through simple acceleration; that idea has been ruled out both theoretically and experimentally. But while the group velocity of a particle-wave train is limited by that of light, the phase velocity is not. Accordingly, in this "future history" the invention of a device for handling discontinuous psi functions permits a spaceship to assume a pseudo-velocity (*not* a true speed in the mechanical sense) limited only by the frequency of the engine's oscillators.

On the basis of this postulated physics, it seems reasonable to suppose that gravity control, both to generate an internal field and as a propulsive mechanism for sub-light travel, is attainable, and that a phenomenon like the "trepidation vortex" may actually exist. Neither assumption is necessary to the plot, but they help it along.

Everything else is strictly within the realm of present science. A blaster gun could be built today, though it would be a large, clumsy machine. (The gun in the story depends on a nearly perfect dielectric, something on which the Bell Laboratories are now working.) Electronic readjustment of an emotional pattern is foreshadowed by such thereapeutic techniques as electric shock and tranquilizing drugs. Our present computers and automata are embryonic robots. Parthenogenesis has already been induced in mammals, and there is no known reason why further research should not make it applicable to man.

Given interstellar travel, there are certain logical social consequences. Men would emigrate to new worlds for one reason or another; in this story, there is no economic motive for leaving Earth, but there is a psychological drive analogous to the wholesale migration of European liberals to America after 1848, in that the majority of men do not find the mechanized, highly intellectualized culture of Earth congenial.

Interstellar war and interstellar government are both improbable: space is too big, an entire planet too self-sufficient. But a loose alliance of the civilized worlds (the Union) and a joint patrol to protect individuals and backward societies from the grosser forms of exploitation (the Coordination Service) are quite likely to be organized. Other features of my future civilization, such as the basic language and the philosophical pantheism of Cosmos—neither one replacing all its older counterparts—are necessarily guesswork; we can only be sure that the future *will* be different from the present. In fact, a story laid some centuries hence must be thought of as a translation, not merely of language but of personalities and concepts corresponding only approximately to anything we know.

Like all new technology, interstellar travel will pose more problems than it solves. Of these, cartography is not the least. Not that anyone in his right mind would bother with three-dimensional maps of the Galaxy; a catalogue of astronomical data is so much hardier. But the Galaxy is so big that numbering each individual star would be a system too clumsy and too prone to error.

I assume instead, that large regions are taken more or

154

less arbitrarily, and that the constellations as they appear from some base planet within each region are named. Thereafter all other stars of the region can be referred to this system of constellations in the usual manner of 20th-century astronomy.

Thus, the Pilot's Manual will catalogue these base planets, or rather their suns, and every such entry will refer you to an entire region. Naturally the larger stars, e.g., Canopus, visible through many regions, will have a different designation in each, but this is a simple matter of cross-reference.

The terrestroid planet Nerthus is such a base. It is about one thousand light-years from Sol in the direction of Argus. The Wolf's Head is a conspicuous constellation in its skies. The proper designation of Atlantis' double sun, translated from Basic to the Latin we use today, is therefore (Ar 293) Delta Capitis Lupi. As in 20th-century astronomical practice, the "Delta" indicates that this star is the fourth brightest in Caput Lupi as seen from Nerthus.

The members of a double star system revolve around their common center of gravity. In practice, the more massive star is chosen as central and called A, its companion B. (Of course, popular names are often given.) The planets of a star are numbered outward, I, II, III, etc., and similarly the moons of any planet.

(I have not *assumed* that nearly every star—of Population I, at least—has planets. This is pretty well-established fact as of 1959.)

The names of bodies within a given system, as opposed to the numbers, are customarily chosen to fit a consistent pattern. The volcanoes and watery outer hemisphere of our world suggested the name Atlantis; mythical Cretan and Greek motifs followed logically for the other bodies, since the Atlantis of legend may well be a dim recollection of the Minoan empire.

Delta Capitis Lupi A (later called Daedalus) is of type AO, a hot bluish star with a mass of four Sols and a luminosity of eighty-one Sols (taken from the mass-luminosity diagram). Its companion B (Icarus) is of type GO, almost identical with Sol. If we regard A as the center, which we may legitimately do, then B revolves about

155

A at an average distance of ninety-eight Astronomical Units with a period of four hundred eighty-five years. From the vicinity of B, A has an apparent luminosity of 0.00085 times that of Sol seen from Earth. This is comparable to Sol at eleven A.U., a way beyond Saturn, but the angular diameter of A at B is much less. To the naked eye at B, A is little more than a super-brilliant star.

A has three planets of its own, none habitable to man. B has two, of which Minos is the first. Otherwise, because of stellar gravitational effects, there are only asteroids.

Minos has an average distance from B of one A.U. Therefore it gets on an average nearly the same amount of heat and light as Earth. However, the gravitational pull of A has elongated this orbit toward itself, so that the ellipse has an eccentricity of 0.2. Hence the seasons on Atlantis, winter coming when Minos is farthest from B and closest to A, summer when these conditions are reversed.

Minos is of the general type of sixty-one Cygni C, the extrasolar planet discovered by Strand in 1944. Its mass is about five thousand times that of Earth, its equatorial diameter fifty-one thousand two hundred kilometers, its rotation period some ten hours. Like all giant planets, it has a dense atmosphere, mostly hydrogen.

It also has eighteen satellites. Most are so small and far out as to be insignificant, but the inner ones are conspicuous from Atlantis, which is the Earth-sized third moon of Minos.

In the table on page 157, Column 1 gives the equatorial diameter of each of the first five satellites, in kilometers. (Their density is about the same as Earth's, 5.5 g/cc.) Column 2 lists the average orbital radius about Minos, in kilometers, Column 3 the period of each orbit in hours. Column 4 shows the angular diameter as seen from Atlantis at closest approach, in degrees of arc. (For comparison, Luna seen from Earth is about 0.5 degree across.) Column 5 lists the time between successive oppositions to Atlantis, in hours. Finally, Column 6 shows the respective names.

All these orbits are ellipses of small eccentricity, approximately in the Minoan equatorial plane though slightly skewed with respect to each other.

156

Moon	1	2	3	4	5	6
I	162	161,000	2.45	Point	3.1	Aegeus
II	3218	272,000	5.2	0.9	9.05	Ariadne
III	12,502	483,000	12.2	—	—	Atlantis
IV	4793	720,000	22.2	0.7	26.9	Theseus
V	1610	1,920,000	97.0	0.07	14.0	Pirithous

The drag of the major planet has given these satellites a period of rotation equal to that of revolution, so that they always turn the same face to their primary. For the same reason, this inner hemisphere is bulged toward Minos and there is little axial tilt, though considerable precession.

In the case of Atlantis especially, this permanent deformation has concentrated most of the land in the inner hemisphere and made the main continent, on and about which the action of the story takes place, extremely mountainous. (Later this continent was named Labyrinth.)

The inner hemisphere of Atlantis has a spectacular sky. Minos shows an angular diameter of about seven degrees and, having an albedo of forty-five percent, is brilliantly luminous, equivalent in full phase to roughly twelve hundred full moons of Earth. In addition, Ariadne and Theseus each give several times as much light as Luna. Aegeus and Ariadne never set, but are seen to move across Minos from west to east, then back again behind Minos in the opposite direction. As Column Five shows, to an observer accustomed to Earth's moon, these satellites would appear almost to hurtle. Aegeus is seen to complete its path through the sky in 3.1 hours and to go through a full cycle of phases in about thirty hours; the apparent path is some eighteen degrees across. This moon, however, shows merely as a small, rapid star of fluctuating brightness. Ariadne completes its apparent path, ca. thirty-two degrees wide, in 9.05 hours and a cycle of phases in about sixty-three and one-half hours or some five Atlantean days. Because of orbital inclination, all the moons are usually "above" or "below" Minos when they pass it. An occasional sight is the full Ariadne transitting the full Minos at midnight and turning a dull coppery hue as it enters the Atlantean shadow cone. The large outer moon Theseus rises and sets in a normal manner, moving a trifle more slowly than Luna, and completes a cycle of phases in about one hundred thirty-five hours or eleven Atlantean days.

The outer hemisphere never sees Minos, sees the inner moons rise and set low in the sky only near the hemispheric boundary, and sees less of Theseus.

The system Ariadne-Atlantis-Theseus begins a new cycle of motions about every three hundred fifty hours.

During the winter half of the Minoan year, which is about as long as Earth's, the companion sun A illuminates Atlantis after B has set. In summer the two stars seem gradually to approach each other, until at mid-summer A is occulted by B.

The inner hemisphere of Atlantis sees a total eclipse of B every day, when the satellite gets Minos between itself and the star. The precise time depends on longitude; it is nearly at noon in the locale of this story. The theoretical duration of this eclipse is about eleven minutes, actually somewhat less because of the refracting effect of the Minoan atmosphere. A is eclipsed sometime during the day in summer and sometime during the night in winter. There are also occasional eclipses of either sun by the other moons.

Ariadne and Theseus have strong tidal effects on the oceans of Atlantis, the first raising tides about equal to those of Earth, the second, tides almost six times as high. In addition, there is the more or less steady influence of Minos and the shifting, weaker effects of B and the smaller moons. This leads to turbulent oceans with fantastically complicated patterns of waves, ebb, and flow. Low shores are turned to salt marshes, high shores whipped by a murderous surf. Tidal bores are very common along the uneven continental shelves. Only inland seas approach terrestrial conditions.

The same gravitational forces make Atlantean diastrophism more rapid than Earth's. The satellite has extensive volcanic regions and few areas are free of earthquakes. The release of carbon dioxide through vulcanism in tectonic eras, followed by its equally rapid consumption in the exposed rock of newly risen mountains, makes the geological history one of sudden climatic shifts. Because of the higher Coriolis force, cyclonic storms on Atlantis are both more frequent and more violent than those of Earth.

At the time of this story, however, there is a mild interglacial climate and the life, whose biochemistry is quite terrestroid—as one would expect on a world so similar to Earth—is flourishing. There are no polar icecaps, but the highest mountains retain a few glaciers and the uplands have snow in winter.

It might seem inevitable that mammals would develop under such changeable conditions, but there is nothing inevitable about evolution. The progress of Atlantean life has, indeed, been retarded by the undependable weather and cataclysmic geology, which tend to kill off new land forms before they can become well-established. Only the birds are equipped to escape changes more sudden and powerful than anything Earth has ever known—and 20th-century geologists are coming to believe that the climatic revolutions of our own planet took place more rapidly than was once thought. Whenever conditions have again become favorable, the Atlantean birds have exploded into a new multiplicity of species, including giant flightless types.

As a matter of fact, there are a few primitive mammals on Atlantis; on the outer hemisphere, where the greater water surface makes the weather a bit more stable. But they have not yet reached the inner section, and the human castaways, unable to sail far on those tricky seas, never see them.

And this is the scientific background of the story. The reader is invited to make his own calculations on the basis of my assumed data, and challenge me if he thinks I've gone wrong anywhere. That's one of the things which makes science fiction fun.